BLOOD LUCK

"What did you hunt for, George? I mean, just what did you get out of it?" the major asked.

The soldier's face was bone-white and little drops of sweat were all over it and he was shaking. George was staring down at the paper. The major looked down, too, and that was when there was the explosion.

The glass in the soldier's hand seemed to explode because the soldier squeezed it.

The next thing would be to jump the major.

What saved the major's life was the hand still outstretched. First it was dripping water and then it was dripping blood. When George saw the blood he forgot there was anyone or anything else there.

Slowly he brought the dripping hand up to his face . . .

"PERHAPS THE MOST SOLID SHOCKER OF THE YEAR . . . NOT FOR THE TIMID!"
—*Buffalo Evening News*

Also by Theodore Sturgeon *available from Ballantine Books:*

MORE THAN HUMAN
NOT WITHOUT SORCERY
E PLURIBUS UNICORN
CAVIAR

SOME OF YOUR BLOOD

Theodore Sturgeon

BALLANTINE BOOKS • NEW YORK

 Published in the United States by Ballantine Books, a division of Random House, Inc., New York, and simultaneously in Canada by Ballantine Books of Canada, Ltd., Toronto, Canada.

ISBN 0-345-25712-X-150

Manufactured in the United States of America

First Edition: January 1961
Third Printing: February 1977

Cover art by George Ziel

SOME OF YOUR BLOOD

. . . . but first, a word:

You know the way. You have the key. And it is your privilege.

Go to the home of Dr. Philip Outerbridge. Go on in—you have the key. Climb the stairs, walk to the end of the corridor, and turn left. This is Dr. Phil's study, and a very comfortable and well-appointed one it is. Books, couch, books, desk, lamp, books, books. Go to the desk—sit down; it's all right. Open the lower right drawer. It's one of those deep, double drawers. It's locked? But you have the key—go ahead.

Pull it open—more than that. All the way. That's it. See all those file-folders, a solid mass of them? Notice how they are held in a sort of box frame? Well, lift it out. (Better get up; it's heavy.) There.

Underneath, lying flat, are a half-dozen folders—just plain file folders. Perhaps they are there to level up the main box-frame; well, they certainly do that. Perhaps, too, they are there because they are hidden, concealed, secret. Both perhapses could be true. And perhaps they are there because they are valuable, now or later. Value is money, value is knowledge, value is entertainment . . . sentiment, nostalgia. Add that perhaps to the others. It does not destroy them. And bear in mind that of the six folders, any of six might be any or all of these things. You may look at one of them. The second one from the top. You will note that it, like the others, is marked with Dr. Outerbridge's name and, in large red capitals, PERSONAL—CONFIDENTIAL—

PRIVATE. *But go ahead. Go right ahead; take it out, replace the box-frame, close the drawer, light the lamp, make yourself comfortable. You may read through the papers in this folder.*

But first rest your hands on the smooth cream-yellow paperboard and close your eyes and think about this folder which is marked CONFIDENTIAL *and which is hidden in a drawer which is locked. Think how it was filled some years ago, when Dr. Phil was a young staff psychologist in a large military neuropsychiatric hospital. It happened that he was then two months short of the required age for a commission, so he rated as a sergeant. Yet he had, since his freshman year in college, trained and interned in psychological diagnosis and treatment at a famous university clinic, where he had earned a graduate degree in clinical psychology.*

It was wartime, or something very like it. The hospital was swamped, staggered, flooded. The staff had to learn as many new tricks, cut as many unheard-of corners, work as unholy hours, as those in any other establishment that handled the goings and comings of war, be they shipbuilders or professors of Baltic languages. And some of the staff, like some builders and teachers everywhere, were burdened by too many hours, too little help, too few facilities, and too much tradition, yet found their greatest burden the constant, grinding, overriding necessity for quality. Some men in tank factories turned down each bolt really tight; some welders really cared about the joints they ran. Some doctors, then, belonged with these, and never stopped caring about what they did, whether it was dull, whether it was difficult, whether, even, the whole world suddenly turned enemy and fought back, said quit, said skip it, it doesn't matter.

So perhaps the value of these folders, and their secrecy lies in their ability to remind. Open one, relive it. Say, here was a triumph. Say, here is a tragedy. Say, here is a terrible blunder for which atonement can never be made . . . but which, because it was made, will never be made again. Say, here is the case which killed me; though I have not died, yet when I do I shall die of it. Say, here was my great insight, my inspiration, one day my book and my immortality. Say, here is failure; I think it would be anyone's failure, I—I pray God I never discover that someone else could succeed with something, some little thing I should have done and did not. Say . . . there is something to be said for each of these folders, guarded once by a lock, again by concealment, and at last by the declaration of privacy.

But open your eyes now and look at the folder before you. On the index tab at its edge is lettered

"GEORGE SMITH"

The quotation marks are heavily and carefully applied, almost like a 66 and a 99.

Go ahead.

Open it.

You know the way. You have the key. And it is your privilege. Would you like to know why? It is because you are The Reader, and this is fiction. Oh yes it is, it's fiction. As for Dr. Philip Outerbridge, he is fiction too, and he won't mind. So go on—he won't say a thing to you. You're quite safe.

It is, it is, it really is fiction. . . .

Here is a typewritten letter written on paper showing signs of having been torn across the top with a straight-edge, as if to remove a letterhead. The letters O-R over the date are in ink, printed by hand, large and clear.

Base Hospital HQ,
Portland Ore.: otherwise known as—
Office of the Understaff O-R
Freudsville, Oregon. 12 Jan.

Dear Phil:

First and foremost notice the O-R notation above. That means off the record, and I mean altogether. If and when you see it in future you don't need explanations. Anything which can be gotten across by abbreviation and in code is a blessing to me, especially since they gave me this nut factory to administer without relieving me of that bedlam of yours. You'll excuse the layman's vulgarisms, dear doctor; believe me, they do me good.

Under separate and highly official cover, and through channels, you'll find orders from me to you relative to a file AX544. I'm the colonel and you're the sergeant. I'm the administrator and you're just staff. Hence the orders. On the other hand we are old friends and you are senior to me in your specialty six times umpteen squared. The fact—not mentioned in the orders—is that we've pulled the kind of blooper you don't excuse by saying oops, sorry. This soldier was yanked out of a staging area overseas and shipped back here with a "psychosis, unclassified" label and a "dangerous, violent" stencil, by a meat-headed MedCorps major. It could only have been sheer vindictiveness, deriving from the fact that the GI punched him in the nose. Criminal he may be—according to the distinctions now current—but insane he is not. Seems to me he did the right thing; but to the major's dim appreciation it appeared insane to strike an officer and so he was sent to your laughing academy instead of to a stockade.

What complicates things is that we lost this guy. What with understaffing and turnover and all-around snafu, this GI has been stuck in padded solitary for three months now without diagnosis or treatment, and if he didn't qualify as one of your charges when he got there, he sure as hell should now.

However, it happened, it comes out looking like the worst kind of carelessness, to say nothing of injustice. So what "diagnose and treat" means in the official order is, please, Phil, on bended knee, get that man out of there and out of the Army in such a way that there will be no kickbacks, lawsuits or headlines. And aside from the merits of the case itself, we have to slough off these trivial cases. We need the bed. *I* need the bed, or will soon if this kind of thing happens again.

I trust you to sew it up tidily, Philip. Not only a sound diagnosis, but a sound-sounding one. And then a medical discharge. His remuneration, whether or not he ever appreciates it, can be that his fisticuffs on the person of that moo-minded major are on the house.

yr absentee landlord,
Al

P.S.: To enrich the jest, I just got word that above-mentioned major, by name Manson, got himself deceased in line of duty, in a C-119 crash. This I learned in answer to my request for any additional files he may have on subject patient. There ain't any files.

A.W.

Here is the carbon copy of a letter.

Field Hospital 2
Smithton Township, Cal.: also called— O-R
Bedpan Bureau 14 Jan.
Reik's Ranch, Cal.

Dear Al:

You diagnose right handily by mail. You must have been studying that technique where the quack sends you a ten-dollar Kleenex and you wipe it over your face and send it back and he tells you you've got housemaid's knee. I spent a half-hour with the guy today—honest to God, Al, all the time I could split off—and I found him up on the top floor all alone in a secure cell. Very polite, very quiet. Although he offers nothing, he responds well. I had no hesitation in holding out some hope to him—all he wants is out, and I handed him the idea that if he cooperates with me he ought to make it. He was pathetically eager to please. For once and probably the only time, I'm glad I'm not an officer. He doesn't like officers. And as you said, if we put in solitary every GI who feels that way we'd have to evacuate the entire state of California for housing.

Not having anything with me on that first visit to do any tests—including time, damn you—I sent Gus for a composition book and some ball-points and told the patient to write the story of his life any way it came to him, suggesting that third person might help. That'll give him something to do until I can get back to him, which will be soon—even sooner if you'll okay a requisition for a thirty-hour day and a sleep-eliminator for me.

yrs wearily,
Phil

The third or fourth carbon of a typed transcription.

George's Account

The first that anybody heard about George was at this big staging area outside Tokyo and they were so busy they threw a lot of work to people who usually didn't do it. Which is the usual Army thing, thousands of guys sitting around waiting and a few dozen knocking themselves out. One of the things was the mail. The mail had to be censored but for military stuff and in this particular war, only certain special military stuff. Anything else was nobody's business but whoever wrote the letter.

All the same some lieutenant who should have known better, well, he did know better but he did it anyway, he got very puzzled at one of the letters he was supposed to censor. He took it to a friend of his who happened to be a major in the Medical Corps, but this major was not just a doctor, he was a psychiatrist. He looked at the letter and told the lieutenant he had no business worrying himself about it, it was not military, which the lieutenant already knew. And that did not do any good because the major had the letter now and it bothered him just as much, so he sent for the soldier who wrote the letter.

The next day the major cleared up his desk and went and opened the door to the little room outside where this soldier was waiting. The major had a file in his hand turned around back to back with a lot of papers. He said "Come in uh," and looked at the papers, "uh Smith."

The soldier came in and the major closed the door. The soldier was at attention but he looked around when he heard the door close. The major did not look at him yet but walked past him looking at the papers and he said "It's all right, soldier. At ease." And he didn't seem to be so tough. He sat down and put the papers on the desk and squared them away and finally he leaned back in his shiny brown swivel chair and took a good look at the soldier.

What he saw was a big fellow with yellow hair and a pink kind of skin and the shoulders and chest that make the shirt look like it grew on him, it was so snug. He had thick arms and thick legs and he kept his face closed.

Up to now the major did not tell the soldier he had the letter. So the soldier did not know why he was there.

The major said, "The company clerk tells me you're something of a loner, Smith. Don't run with a crowd much."

The soldier just said, Yes sir. He always liked to let the other guy do the talking as much as he could.

"What do you do for amusement?"

"I like to walk around. At home I fish some. Hunt." The major did not say anything to this so the soldier had to say, "There isn't much of that here. Coons and chucks, I mean. Rabbits."

The major looked down at his papers and said, "Miss that a lot?"

"Well, yes sir, I reckon."

"Got a girl at home, George?" The Major called him George this time.

"Sure do, yes sir."

"Go in town once in a while, do you?"

George knew just what he meant and he just shook his head no.

The major picked up a paper and looked to see if it had anything written on the other side, which it had not. It was blue paper and had two lines written on it.

It was only then that George began staring at it. He stared at it as much as the major did for the rest of the time he was there but from farther off. The major seemed to be going to say something about the paper but he did not. He said, "What do you hunt for, George? I mean, just what do you get out of it?"

He waited, looking down at the paper, and when he did not get an answer he looked up to the soldier's face. Then he said, real soft and long, "Hey-y-y . . ." and got on his feet. He went to the far corner of the room quickly but sort of sidling, watching the soldier's face the whole time, took down a glass, filled it from a cooler, came back and passed it to the soldier. The major said, "Here, you better drink this."

The soldier's face was bone-white and little drops of sweat were all over it and he was shaking and his eyes were half-way closed and what they call glazed. He took the glass but he did not seem to know he was taking it. He did not drink out of it but just held it out in front of him. He was staring down at the paper. The major looked down there too and that was when there was the explosion.

The glass, it seemed to explode but that was really because the soldier squeezed it. The next thing would be to jump the major and the major knew that because he turned just as white as the soldier. But what saved the major's life was the hand still out. First it was dripping water and then it was dripping blood. The blood dripping was what saved the major, because when George Smith saw it he like forgot there was anyone or anything else there. Slowly he brought his hand up to his face. The fingers opened and pieces of bloody glass fell out. He closed the fist and brought it close and began to smell it. He opened it and along the outside edge of the hand under the little finger, blood was pulsing where a little artery was cut. George put his mouth on that part.

The major must have pushed a button under his desk or something because the door banged open without knocking and two MP's ran in and grabbed George. After a while the major had to come and help, and then two more MP's came and that did it. The major had a bloody nose and one of the MP's just lay there on the floor without moving. George got his hand back to his mouth and stood breathing like a bull through his nostrils and watching the blood on the major's face.

"Wait a minute," the major said when the MP's started hustling the soldier out, and they stopped. He looked George Smith straight in the eye and spoke to him kindly. He was breathing hard and bleeding but he really was kindly. He said, "What was it, soldier? What did I say?"

George looked at the file folder on the desk and then he looked at the major bleeding and he sucked at his bleeding hand, and he did not say anything. For three months he did not say anything because he figured he had said much too much already.

They packed up the file folder and the soldier and sent both back Stateside.

This George Smith was twenty-three years old at the time. He came from Kentucky, back in the hills. It was hills with woods and hills with farms and every once in a while these little towns that grow like you know, hair, around something, crossroads or a hole in the ground like a mine.

George came from a mine town. His mother and father came from the old country. They got married on this side. The father was working in Charleston, South Carolina when he met the mother. Probably the only reason he married her was she was the only girl he knew who could talk to him. There sure was nothing else worth while between them. Lonely. People get lonesome by theirselves and then get hooked up and go off and be lonesome together.

When they went to Kentucky so he could work in the mines they were always set apart from everybody because they never did learn much English. Whatever it was he wanted, friends or some place to belong or to be a big shot, he tried to find in a bottle. About the earliest thing George could remember was the father bellowing drunk and the mother screaming and sometimes George screaming too. This was not the kind of memory like a thing happens and you remember it. This was no special one time, but like a colored light or a smell that you live in all the time. And hungry. Practically all the time hungry. Hungry waiting for the father to come home and sometimes he didn't and sometimes he came late and one single word to him about it and he'd start slugging. You found out that when the mother yelled you didn't feel hungry any more.

But all the same it was nice. Like the woods. You could walk in the woods and know where you were, first a little way away from the house, then more, finally, anywhere. The woods in the rain, in the snow, the woods even when you were hungry, they couldn't hurt you the way you might get hurt at home. You might die in the woods or get killed, but the woods did not drink, the woods did not punch your mother in the face. You're always all right if you can get away into the woods. The woods are smooth, you might say, towns are rough. You can lay up to the smooth woods and drink, but not towns, not people, all split halfway up and prickly. Also you know where you stand in the woods. Animals, now, they never stay mad. You go to club a rabbit and you miss, or hurt him and he gets away, he's not going to get sore about it. Maybe he's learned something and maybe he's more careful after that, more scared, but that's all. But if you hit out at a person you never know what's going to come of it, from nothing at all all the way down to a stretch in the Big House. Also if a squirrel should see you cut a squirrel, it makes no never mind. But if a person sees you cut a person, look out. Even years later.

When George was old enough to walk he was old enough to be in the woods. No matter what happened they were there waiting for him. From the time he was eleven there was something as good, even better, because the father's sister married a man who had a farm in the south part of Virginia and although it was a long way away he got to go there once in a while. And he found out years later that as farms go that farm was pretty nothing, but at the time it was heaven. And for a while he lived there permanent. But that was later after everyone died.

The only really bad thing that ever happened to George in the woods was when he was five and he heard voices and crawled up a ridge and looked down and saw a guy giving it to a girl. It was not the first time he had seen it but this was different from what happened at home because the girl was not crying. What he always remembered most about it was this girl's ankles, they were in the air and every time the guy lunged they wiggled like putty. George was watching this not thinking one way or the other about it when the other guy—there was two of them taken this girl out in the woods and the one was hanging around waiting—well this second guy come up behind George and whupped him with a tree trunk. It was not a very big tree and it was a long time dead and punky or I guess George would be dead but it hurt a lot and also scared him very bad, the guy running after him whupping him eight or ten times till George got away the brush being so thick around there and him so small, it was like clubbing a rabbit in brambles, you just can't do it.

They say that these things affect you in late life but it never bothered George. I mean if it was supposed to scare him away from the woods it did not. Even at five years old George could understand that it was not the woods done it to him.

Well George had to go to school like everybody else and that was where he first learned to let other people do the talking because they all did it so easy. George could talk all right, his father made him do it like in the store and all, but for a long time that hunky talk lay in his mouth and put a stink on every word that came out and they laughed. Of course after a while George could talk American as good as anyone but by that time the whole town was calling the father the town drunk which he was and any time George opened his mouth he was like to get somebody's fist in it. And besides the other kids in town used to run together all the time and go to each other's house, but nobody ever came to George's house because that was the one and only place they were scared of the father. And besides the mother was always too sick and too tired. She had the arthritis at first in her hands and it hurt her to do the wash and clean up although she did as much as she could and George helped her when nobody was watching. But one thing he would not do was hang out the clothes because the kids one time saw him do it.

All this could of been worse because George just naturally grew big, sixteen pounds when he was born, his mother used to say that's what gave her the arthritis, then from the time he was eight or so he really grew and what with getting left back in school two years he was always bigger than the kids he was thrown in with. By the time he was twelve he was six feet and a hundred and seventy pounds.

About the hunting. He was only about seven or eight when he started to get anywhere good at it. A sling shot was all right but it took a long while to get good at. Sometimes he could bean a rabbit with a club. You go out in the early morning when it is dark and be there at the edge of a field by the woods when the first light comes. You have a club about two feet long and thick as your wrist, green maple or hickory is best, green because it is heavier that way. Pine is easier to cut but it gets that pitch on your hands and clothes and you can not get it off. You get yourself set in thick brush but near the edge so your arm can swing clear. You stand with your arm back and the club resting in a tree crotch or some place that takes the weight of it and you make up your mind you will be there without moving for a good long time. Pretty soon it begins to get light and then the rabbits come out and eat the clover and timothy or whatever, and jump around and lay flat and rub their stomachs on the wet grass and all that. You pick out your rabbit and you make up your mind no other one will do. No matter how close another one comes you leave it be. Pretty soon your rabbit will get just where you want him and no matter what he does, roll over, wave his feet in the air, squat down and nibble, sniff around another rabbit or whatever, you leave him be. But when he holds real still with all four feet on the ground and his chin down and his ears floppy, because when his ears are up he's on lookout, then you let fly with your club. You want to scrape it away from the tree it is resting on because that makes a little sound, just enough to bring him straight up on his haunches. He's sticking up out of the ground like a boundary peg. You scrape your club off the tree and throw it all at once, no waiting, and you throw it low and fast, level with the ground and no higher than the middle of his ears and you throw it so it spins like an airplane propeller (but the airplane would have to be flying straight up) and you jump out and dive on that rabbit as soon as the club leaves your hand. Now if the club hits right it likes to tear his head plumb off but if it knocks him going away, or if it gets him on the shoulder, it just like stuns him and you better be there to grab him because he can be stunned and back on his feet and gone before you can blink. And if he is stunned you can grab him and you take hold of his two hind legs in your left hand and pick him up and when you do that to a rabbit he straightens right out and throws his head back, so with your right hand you chop straight down with the edge of it and it breaks his neck and he never moves and blood runs out of his nose. But if you do that to a rat or a chuck or a coon or a squirrel it will not straighten out and throw up its head but instead it will curl up the other way and bite you. A squirrel can bite you nine times before you can say ouch and it has big yellow teeth an inch long. A rat that looks dead can get you if you hold it even by the end of the tail, it can climb up that tail with its front feet hand over hand and cut you good before you get sense enough to let go. A squirrel bites straight down and leaves holes as big as his teeth but a rat has a way of slashing, the hole is always much bigger than his teeth, you can not figure out how he does it. A rat if he is stunned you want to grab the end of his tail and put your foot on it crosswise so the tail is under the arch of your foot and then pull him up close to the shoe on the other side of the foot. That way you got him up tight where he can't but lash around some and you have one hand free to club him or pick up a rock or your knife or stomp him with your other foot. A ground squirrel, what they call back East a chipmunk, is not worth your trouble, he has a tail comes off if you grab it, well it does not come off but it skins off and he gets away and the rest of the tail shrivels up and drops off later. A chipmunk can bite worse than a rat almost and you would not believe anything that size could get his mouth open that wide, and once you got him what have you got? He has no more juice than a stewed prune. A skunk is not worth your trouble, although they are easy to get because they are not afraid of nothing. A possum all you have to do is lift him clear of the ground. A coon you want to have a good club for and you do not do nothing but club him and keep it up till you are sure, if he ever gets his back against a tree or a rock and he is not dead yet you will think somebody threw a buzz saw at you spinning. George got a bobcat throwing a club once but never again. All cats got the same taste, you breathe outward through your nose and there's a taste there like cat pee smell. For hours. You wouldn't believe it but snakes taste all right, maybe a little fishy but there is nothing wrong with fish, the only thing is it is not warm. Birds are a waste of time they are mostly feathers, except a couple of times George saw wild turkey but he never did get near enough for even a big sling shot. Except ducks. Ducks are fine.

When George got a little older, ten or eleven, he got good with traps. He never could pay for steel traps but he got so good with snares he did not need them. He could make a deadfall big enough to take a badger and that is saying something because a badger can dig straight down through a blacktop road if he has to unless your deadfall rock is big enough to kill him first crack, but this George was a strong boy. Your deadfall is nothing but a big flat rock tipped up and propped on a stick. Some people tie a long string to the stick and wait and watch all day till something goes under the rock after the bait, but that is for boy scouts. George liked to prop up the rock and then whittle the stick almost through, and tie the string to the notch. The string goes back under the rock around a peg sunk in the ground and then back a ways and you tie your bait to it. A fox or a possum will grab hold and pull, and the stick breaks and down comes the rock. For rabbits a carrot is the best bait because it is strong. For foxes or even a badger sometimes rabbit meat is good, but don't ever use the kidneys or you will catch yourself some kind of damn cat.

The nicest one of all is the figure-four, and George could make one faster than you can climb a yellow pine tree. All you do is find a nice young hardwood sapling, ash or hickory or even birch if you got to. You pace off the right distance, depends on the tree, and dig a hole. Then you find a branch thick as your thumb with a good V crotch on it. You cut it through right under the V and then you cut away one of the side branches leaving a spur. What you have now is a bushy branch with a hook like. You turn this upside down and bury the branchy part, stomping it good and putting heavy rocks in the hole and maybe a log on top, so just the upside-down hook is showing out of the ground. You cut a little notch in the shank part of the hook and whittle yourself a good strong double-pointed peg to fit into that notch and cross to the tip of the hook. It looks like a figure 4.

Now you pull down your sapling to bend almost double and tie a piece of twine near the top and the other end of the twine to the double-pointed peg, and set the peg in the hook to make the figure 4. Real easy you let the bent tree pull up until the peg sets hard against the hook. Now, tied to this twine just above the figure 4 is another piece of twine, and tied to this is nothing in the world but a old number one guitar string, the kind with a little bitty brass stopper on one end looks like a hollow brass barrel. You have the end of the guitar string passed through this to make a loop. You lay this loop around the bait, and you tie the bait with a short cord to the double-ended peg in the figure 4. You shake fine dirt all around until the loop is buried and the bait-cord is buried, and then you go home. In the morning you got yourself a rabbit or a chuck or maybe even a fox or badger. Because first time he tugs on the bait he pulls out the peg and that snaps upright and that thin wire loop grabs him and hangs him up higher than Haman. Or maybe it's a damn skunk or maybe nothing but the chawed off foot of a fox, but usually it's something good.

Oh this George he loved to hunt. But he never liked killing anything. He had no use for people who killed things just to be killing when the animals never did nothing to them. Nobody should kill nothing they don't need to for some purpose. Like deer. One time George found a doe pressed flat against the ground by a fallen tree after a bad windstorm and he worked all morning clearing it away with just a bitty hand axe and dragging up poles until he could lever it up high enough to let the deer out. The doe like to died of fear but George just laughed and went on working till he got it loose. George never did kill a deer. They are too big anyway. But this George, when he wasn't hunting, or maybe fishing, he was laying around thinking about it. He sure did like to do it.

All the time this hunting was going on, and school days and all, things were getting worse around the house. The mother got more arthritis and pretty soon she stopped cleaning the house much and couldn't hardly cook even. This made the father mad and he got worse than ever. Sometimes he was out all night and would go to work drunk in the morning and he was a good worker, strong, but sometimes when the foreman would say something he would argue back and once he hit him but not much. So he kept getting laid off. When he got laid off he would draw his pay and then he would go on a mad drunk until he spent it all. It was not too bad when he stayed away at those times but when he came home it was very bad. George and the mother always tried not to say the one word that would set him off but any word would do it. Then he would beat up the mother, punching her right in the face and the blood came and the mother cried but she never screamed real loud she was so ashamed. He used to beat up George too but when George was big enough to run away he would run away as soon as the trouble started and even before that, as soon as the father came home. He would come back after the father was asleep. Once the father was asleep there was never any more trouble and when he woke up he never seemed to remember anything about it. George never ran to the neighbors because they had no use for any of them or to the cops because the father hated cops and George never thought there was anything wrong with that, who was to tell him different? He just went into the woods and lay up in a tree or hunted if it was moonlight or maybe just hung around outside until it got quiet and then peeked in the window to see if he was asleep and if he was he would come in and get in bed.

And sometimes he would already be in bed and even asleep when the father came in and those were the times he would wake up hearing the mother crying, first, "Don't, don't, not now, the boy, the boy," and the father would growl that the boy was asleep. George would keep his eyes tight closed and lie still like in the woods waiting for the rabbits, and the mother crying "no no" until she would give a little scream and say, "My hands, oh, my hands," because that is what he would do, squeeze her arthritis until she gave in, because he always said there was nothing really wrong with her, she was faking. So she would stop saying no no but go on crying until he went to sleep. That was one thing about it, he always went right to sleep.

When George was thirteen he was as big as a man. He was as big as his father and maybe stronger although he did not seem to know this. His father was a yellow headed man with a lot of bad teeth and his skin hung down under his eyes with like little bloody hammocks under the eyeballs and his pants fit him best if he let his stomach hang out over his belt so he always wore them real low like that. When George was a little kid he used to try to wear his pants like that but he never had the belly for it. When he got bigger he stopped trying to do anything like the father. Well when he was thirteen something happened that changed everything.

The father had been working for quite a spell and for a while there was plenty to eat and George helped out as much as he could with the cleaning up and all. Because the father would come home and when he was sober and the house was all cleaned up and dinner cooking he maybe wasn't like a kind and loving husband in the movies but at least he walked in and washed up and ate and sat in the door whittling and went to bed without yelling at anybody or hitting. And once or twice he would look at something George did like white-washing the wall or fixing the busted porch rail or a step or something and he would look at it and at George and he would say "Wal aw kay!" in that foreign accent of his and George would of done anything for him then. And he could still remember the one time he came in and sniffed in the kitchen and said, "Poy, dat schmells goot!" and the mother just sat there in her wheelchair and cried. She got the wheelchair from the priest who came visiting I guess to see if a wheelchair would make her or George or even the father go to church once in a while, but they never did, the father told them not to and cussed every time he saw the wheelchair for a month but all the same he let her keep it.

And with things that way naturally George and the mother knocked themselves out trying to keep everything nice to make it last as long as they could and make the father glad to come home to a nice place. So this one night was the day he was supposed to stop off at the store on the way home because they were out of food pretty much but for a slab of fatback and some turnip greens. The mother set that aside for some other time and her and George got everything ready for the father to come home with the food, and they talked it around this way and that what they'd fix according to what he brought, so they could have it ready real quick, like if he had a lump of chuck they'd slice off some and quick pound it with the edge of a plate to make pan-fry steaks with onions if he brought onions, or if he brought collards they wouldn't boil them but sear them quick in hot fat. George always felt very close to his mother but in a funny way disappointed or something like that. Like when she got sorry for herself and used to cry and tell him how she caught the arthritis from him being born and she would pat herself on her skinny chest and say how hard she tried to feed him off her own body but she couldn't he was too big and she was too sick and how she wished she could. It was like she was always feeding him from herself all his whole life, and what she put out, it cost her, it weakened and sickened her, but still she did it and did it. For him. And at the same time it was like he needed something from her, he took what she fed him, but it was never enough and it was never the right thing that he wanted. It is very hard to explain this. But anyway he always felt her giving and giving out of herself, and he always needed something from her, and hung around her to get it, only what she was giving him all the time was not the thing he wanted. This would get so bad with him sometimes that he would have to go hunting again. That usually made him feel better.

But now this one time when they were waiting for the father to come home and planning all the different things they might be doing to fix something quick and good for him it began to get later and later and they talked a little more to cover it up and then they got quiet and just waited, she was in her wheelchair looking down at her hands, her hands by now were all brown and twisted like cypress. And George he sat in the doorway looking down the cowpath that ran down to the road where the father would have to come. And when it got dark the mother said as bright as she could, "I know! Just shave up that fatback and we'll fry it up like bacon and have bacon sandwiches and we can boil up a lump of it with the turnip greens and then I think there's a little beans left too. A whole dinner, and we can have it all ready!" So George got right up out of the doorway, it was beginning to get too dark to see anyway, and he lit the kerosene lamp and shook up the stove and went to the table with the knife and the fatback to shave it up. So that is how he come to have the knife at the time. He did not go for it and he wouldn't never even thought about it except there it was in his hand.

In walked the father and he was drunk as a hoot-owl and he looked all around the place and said "Gaw dam dot Polock," and that was all we needed to know, he had fought with the foreman and got laid off and drew his money and got drunk. And the mother she just couldn't hold it in, she let out one long wail and threw up her poor crooked hands and said oh, oh again, again, and he run right through the room and punched her one in the nose so hard you could hear it break and the blood squirted out before he could get his hand away. So George clear across the room, he never could remember afterward actually doing it, he threw the knife.

Well it was so quiet in there for so long you wouldn't believe it. Then the father peeled off his undershirt which was all he was wearing besides pants, it was a hot day, and he looked down at the cut and the blood coming out of it. And the mother was bleeding through her hands and her eyes bulging out over them, looking at the father. And the father pushed George away and got the dishrag and splashed cold water on his chest and wiped it with the dish towel and got his other undershirt from the peg over the bed and a clean rag and put the rag against the cut and pulled the shirt on over it and went out. Nobody had said word one since he said Gaw dam Polock.

Well nothing was ever the same after that. The father still had money when he left and he drank that all up that same night. The next day he got George alone and talked to him, he said he got drunk first because he was so mad about the layoff, and after what happened he got drunk because he was so sorry. It seemed to make a lot of difference to him that George should understand this but George did not understand it and just shrugged his shoulders. And he did not say he was sorry he threw the knife or anything else and the father did not ask him to as a matter of fact he never mentioned the knife or anything else.

But he never again laid a hand on the mother. He spent most of the time just sitting in the open doorway looking down the cowpath. In a day or two all the fatback and turnip greens was gone and the beans and a heel of bread, but still the father sat in the doorway and the mother in her wheelchair with wet cloths to her nose. Nobody wanted to say anything to the father about getting some food in or going to work so the third day George came back from school and he was carrying a big sack of groceries. He walked right past the father and came in and put the bag down. The part of the bag where George had been holding it against his chest was marked in big black grease pencil Morosch which was the name of a white collar guy in the mine office. George quick took everything out of the bag and shoved the bag in the stove to burn up. Then he put everything out of sight, a roasting chicken and two pounds of hamburger and a loaf of stale for stuffing and a loaf of fresh, two quarts of milk, fresh carrots, a whole pound of butter, a jar of strawberry jam, a pound of coffee and some bananas.

The mother probably was too sick to notice, what with her big shut blue black eyes and her nose three times as big. The father came in and looked at the stuff as George put it away out of sight. "Ware ya gat dat?" he wanted to know.

George for once in his life turned and looked the father straight in the eye. "Swiped it, off the Acme store delivery wagon," and it was the truth. If the father yelled or hit out or said nothing or flew to the moon, just then he did not care.

The father stood for a long time quiet and then made a funny little smile. He said, "Mabbe ya amoont ta schomthing yat, boy." And you know that made the boy George feel better than anything in his whole life, and that's crazy. Because if ever he hated anything it was the father. If ever there was a man he didn't give a damn what he thought, it was the father. But when the father smiled and said that he got all hot in the mirror over the sink he was all pink and to save his soul he couldn't keep from smiling too.

Well the father went back to work after a while, as a swamper out at the head of the slag-pile where they never could keep a man working for long, who wants to be in hell until he is dead? but the father could get back there any time. And things went on quiet, never another drunk, never much talk, and school let out, and the mother sat quieter and quieter. It was like she had quit, she was not going to fight anything any more, him or being ashamed or dirt in the house or anything. She got thin and light as a dead possum, George could easy carry her out to the outhouse and stand her up in there where she would slowly close the door and after a long time he would hear her calling and he would go back and she would be standing there and he would carry her back in to her wheelchair. George made a pass at cleaning up when he thought about it. He felt like hunting almost all the time now but he got stubborn inside and wouldn't, just hung around her all the time. After the black eyes went away and the nose was only crooked not swole up they sent for the district nurse and she come and looked at the hands and clucked some and said she had ought to go to the hospital over to Mountaindale but the mother said no! real sharp, the first thing she said in a long while. The nurse took the arm and rolled up the sleeve and looked at it, it was like two peeled willow sticks stuck together, she tried easy to bend the arm and straighten it, it wouldn't go but a little way each way and the mother like gasped and bit on her tongue. So the nurse shrugged again and left some pills for her to take if she was in pain. The mother died about four months after she was hit in the nose. The father went to work that day but George just hung around and hung around and when the wagon came for her he wanted to ride in it and when they wouldn't let him he ran all the way behind it to the funeral home and hung around there until they chased him away. At night he waited until everyone went away and then got around the back and broke in and said goodbye to her in his own way. He swore they would be together one way or the other no matter what. In the morning he was there outside waiting and he hung around until they finished with her and went out to the graveyard. The father came too. They stood side by side watching the grave get filled in and like someone said they looked as if they did not understand it, and they did not. Nobody cried. Afterward the father went back to the mine and George was supposed to go back to school but he went hunting. He did not catch anything. That was the bad part.

•

Life went on, George was hunting a lot of the time and the father working and the funny part of it was the father began to straighten out a little at least as far as the drink went. He worked steady and they gave him a job at the shaft checking tools and if he kept on that way he'd wind up down below making real money for a change. But he did not want that, or anyway he did not try for it. The crazy thing was that for the first time anyone could remember he did things around the house. Not much but the whole time his wife was alive he never set hand to a broom unless to hit somebody with it nor got his hands wet except to wash them. Now when it didn't make no difference to anybody he would shove the dirt and beer cans out in the yard every day or so and even scrape off the dishes and rinse them. Once he told George he thought a garden where they could grow some corn and radishes and stuff would be nice only he had no hoe, so George swiped him one off the sidewalk display in front of Mountain Hardware, and the father took it and cussed and cussed, but wagging his head and grinning, he must have knew George swiped it because where would George get money? but he never asked, he was just pleased and he actually hoed out a patch and George went in the Acme and pretended to be studying the seed pictures and swiped eight packs of seeds, corn and melon and sunflowers and some hot peppers and the father planted them all.

One time at night George was coming home from the old quarry on the other side of town where some big frogs were and right in the middle of town someone came out of an alley and grabbed his arm and he almost hit him but saw it was the father. The father walked along with him and began talking something about we don't have to live like pigs no more if he didn't have to spend all his money for food he would have money for maybe a rug for the floor and some more dishes and a tub to wash them in and another lamp and some paint and things. When they reached the corner the father turned George around and they started back, the father still mumbling on and on about this and when they came to the alley he looked up and back and all around and then quick pulled George into the alley. They went halfway down and it was real dark and the father took George's wrist and pulled his hand down to where it touched one of those slanty cellar doors that comes out the side of some buildings, and the father pulled up on it and it came open a ways and George saw it was not locked. The father lowered it down real quiet and walked off in the dark leaving George standing there. After a while George tried it himself and it opened and he went down the steps. Down there he could not see anything but he could smell the flour and dried prunes and all the other stuff that was there, it was the basement of the Acme market.

The next day he got matches and then in the night he went back and got his pockets full of two cans of milk and a can opener and some tallow candles and best of all a toy flashlight and batteries to fit it, a little tiny thing but all he needed down there. After that he went there every night almost and brought stuff home but he was smart and never took but from open cartons and never left anything around like wrappers or burned matches, and he was always sure to sit quiet under the alley door listening the way he'd do in the woods. The father never said nothing while he slowly filled the whole place up, all the cupboards and under the sink with canned goods and pancake mix and rice and lentils and what all. There was not much said between him and the father but things were better between them than ever before, and sure enough the father did go ahead and spend some money on a little rug for the middle of the floor and some dishes from the five and dime.

So then he found the meat market had a side cellar door too only it was locked. He hung around town a couple of days until the delivery truck came and he helped the man unload cases of bacon and four quarters of beef and four sides of pork, and by the time he made his third trip up and down the stairs he saw where he could jam the spring lock open with a bit of cardboard and he did. That night he went down into the basement and up into the meat market, had a good look up and down the streets outside, then went and opened the walk-in freezer. When he opened the door a big bright light went on inside and scared him so much he slid inside and slammed the door to hide it. As soon as it closed the light went out and when he turned back to the door he couldn't find any handle to open it with. If it had been a Saturday he sure would of been dead Monday morning. As it was he was alive but stiff as a popsicle when they opened up the next day, and the silly thing about it was the door opened with a foot pedal beside the door so the butcher could come out with his hands full but how was a guy supposed to know that in the pitch dark because he forgot his flashlight?

They put him in the lockup and got him thawed out and a couple days later Judge Manorora sent him up for two years, breaking and entering and attempted burglary. The father was there looking like at the funeral as if he did not understand what was going on and there was some whispering and pointing and nodding heads between the judge and the priest who gave the mother the wheelchair and the district nurse who showed up too. The father just sat there, he probably didn't catch one word in ten. George didn't say anything either because after he was thawed out he somehow just didn't care what happened. So the two years wasn't such a tough rap after all because it was in a orphanage kind of place instead of a pen. Nobody ever did find out about the stuff from the Acme market.

Now the thing that George wanted to laugh at, but he was so surprised at it he couldn't laugh, was the one building they put him in first had bars on the windows and no doorknobs just keyholes and a cyclone fence around it with five strands of barbwire on top leaning in and watchtowers at the corners and a small gate in the front with no knob just keyholes and a big gate in the back for trucks, it was a double set so the truck could go in one and get locked in, then they would open the second. The whole time he was there they never did close both sets and he never did see anyone up in the little corner watchtowers, but what was funny was the idea that anyone would want to run away from a place like that.

Everybody had a bed of their own with a clean sheet and a clean blanket and two shelves and a closet with a brown curtain for a door to put things in. Between every bed was a board partition so that except it was open at the end away from the window, once you were in there it was like a little room of your own. In between each two beds, out in the long hallways where the open ends were, was a little wash sink, no kidding, one for each two beds, and hot water as well as cold. For each four beds there was a toilet across the hallway and a stand-up urinal and even if there was no door on it who needs it? At night one guard and two trusties watched each hallway on each floor, six hallways altogether. They had soft rubber shoes but you could hear them coming all the same.

First thing in the morning big bright lights come on and everybody jumps up and puts pants on and comes yammering out to wash the face and brush the teeth and go to the john, with the guards and trusties spaced down to the hallway with a pad and pencil to write your number if you horse around or skip the toothbrushing or forget to wash your hands again after you come out of the can. Downstairs you'd go two by two, no running no pushing, and there was like a damn big restaurant but with nothing to pay. You got to your seat and stood there until the matron, that was a fat woman, said grace and you bent your head down and when she was done you sat down and these trusties brought these big platters of scrambled eggs and whole buckets of hot cocoa to ladle into your tin mug. Barbwire? George thought right away it must be to keep people out, not in. Maybe the dried eggs, because that is what they were, did get old after a few months, but how many times did he go to school or off to the woods with no breakfast at all with the father passed out drunk and the mother sick and crying?

Downstairs along with the restaurant place—they could show movies in it too and church and all—there was a barber shop and a first-aid station like a two-room hospital and a whole row of what they called connies which were consultation rooms for when someone wanted to talk to a guy private like a doctor or a priest or a mother or some other stranger, and the kitchens and a row of offices. This was the one building, three stories high, with the fence around it, and that's where you went first. After a while when they figured you knew your way around they moved you to another building and it was only two stories and it had no fence. They had five like that, all alike. They had no offices in them and only a couple connies and a one-room first-aid station. In each one, one of the connies was made over to a library. Each building had a real piano and its own ball team and like that, with a world series every year. Every day was school from 8 to 12 and then lunch and then school from 2 to 4. Every day half of each building had to work in the fields 4:30 till sundown or 6 in winter. And if you want to know how they got the work done without any dogging-it, each building had its own field and they kept score on how much corn or tomatoes or whatever each one brought in and if you think that world series was fought, boy, you should see them kids pull weeds. There was also shop training for carpentry, electric shop, sheet metal and the bakery.

Now everybody in that place had to gripe because they took you for queer if you did not. But I will bet you the sweat off mine against the sweat off yours that not one in a hundred of those guys lived as good as that where he came from. It was like the fashion to gripe, that's all. Also to make as much noise as possible about how horny you were and where do they keep the dancing-girls. George wished he had a nickel for every ten thousand times those little punks talked about women, but you had to do it. And somebody was always in trouble for making grabs at the pansies or the ones they thought were pansies or the ones they wished were pansies. Most of them wouldn't know what to do if a pansy said yes even if they knew they wouldn't get caught which they would.

George really liked it there. Not that he ever said that, the whole place would macerate anyone who said that. Maybe it was just George. First of all he was big so he didn't get pushed around. Next, any time in his whole life he had been with kids they were all from his town and they all knew about him and his drunk father and his mother couldn't talk English so good, and him getting left back in school and all. In this place, nobody ever heard of him before and all they knew was he was up for burglary when most of them all they did was their parents didn't want them or died or something. Next thing, everybody wore the same kind of clothes and slept in the same kind of bed, so what did they have to brag about? While back home, this kid had a bicycle and that one new shoes and the other's father was personnel manager at the mine. Next thing: school. Any kid who was well along in school before he came just went right on with it. But any kid who was behind—especially kids like George who were really behind because they got pushed one way or another and not because they were natural born dumb, well a guy like that got special time in the connies and a real chance to catch up with his age. George was really surprised by this school thing, he didn't know school was that easy and that interesting too, he thought school was a place to tie you up out of the way most of the day and make it easy for them to catch you whatever you did. Here they showed him things he really did not know and should of, like just why it was the poles he used one time could lift a heavy tree off a deer, and also things he could use just as well as a figure-four trap, like how to wire six buttons and four bells so the buttons control the bells you want them to, and when to knock down bread when it was rose enough with the yeast. Last of all, why George liked it there, had a lot to do with George what he was and nothing or nobody else. George kept his mouth shut. George always kept his mouth shut from when he was a little boy, at first because he was scared or shamed to open it and later because it was just too much trouble to get people to understand and at last because he just got the habit. Now most of the people in the world who are in trouble are liars. The wisest thing anyone ever said about lying is this, that to tell the truth is the best because if you tell the truth you never have to remember what it was you said. Well even better than to tell the truth is to keep your mouth shut. If you lie someone is going to make you try to prove it. If you brag, even with the truth, someone is going to call you and you got to make good. If you say anything at all there is bound to be someone listening who don't understand you or who don't hear you right. There would be a whole lot less trouble for everybody if most people just did not talk so much. These are things that George thought a lot about when he was grown and not when he was fourteen in that place, but that's the way he acted anyway, he kept his mouth shut. He never got the habit of running with anyone special either, so he could keep himself to himself. So all the time if he figured out something was good for him he done it. He did not try it out on anybody else and he did not make speeches about it so somebody could maybe talk him out of it. Because there are a lot of people around who can talk real good but do not know very much, they could win an argument about if you should breathe.

Anyway, you can learn a lot more with your mouth shut. You open your mouth you block your ears.

About some things you should have some way to block your ears. If George was out by himself he would not have to listen to all that talk about screwing and everything. Every day, every minute somebody was talking about that. George had seen enough screwing to last him a good long time, he did not have to wonder about it which is what most of those guys were really doing. At the same time it was while he was at the school he changed from a boy into a man and he felt it. He felt it more than he should because of all that talk. He finally put his mind to it and thought it through, lying in bed nights. And it was a long time before he got that thinking finished, but the way it turned out was this.

Being able to shoot your load did not make you nothing special because every rabbit could do it.

Shooting your load maybe was more fun than crapping or peeing but when you come right down to it it is not so special because you don't have to make yourself do it—you can't help it. You wait long enough and it's just naturally going to bust loose, like when you are asleep; you couldn't stop it if you wanted to just like sooner or later you got to go to the john whether you want to or not. So it's nothing anybody has to work at or worry over, which is what all that talk does. If the pressure builds up and you don't want to wait, go get rid of it. You usually go to the john before you absolutely have to too.

But the number one top thing about sex is something that George always felt, somehow, but only figured out much later when he was grown. He figured out that everything that is alive in the whole world keeps taking things in and then working them over and then throwing out what it could not use. No matter what a living thing is doing, what it lives for is the taking in part. It does that first and then it works it over and then it gets rid of the exhaust. Taking in is why it goes and why it grows and how it grows too. No matter how good it feels or how much talk there is about it or how many laws get passed, you can't duck the one thing, that sex is part two not part one. It's one of the things you leave behind you while you go ahead. When they got General Science in the school and it come to Biology George memorized a line in the book, no living organism can exist in an environment of its own waste products. And thinking about that and trying to find words to hang it to, he come up with this and it finished the subject for always, that the first part, taking-in, gives you Satisfaction and the second part, throwing-out, gives you Relief. There is a whole lot of people in the world sick and crazy too who do not know that difference. They go all around looking for relief and then they get upset when it don't satisfy. Well of course it don't satisfy, it can't. Satisfaction is ahead, all what you need to keep you going if you are going to be alive. Relief is what you get by dropping what you don't need any more. It's behind you and if you want to go chasing back to pick it up, don't be surprised if you look a little crazy and get yourself stunk up some too.

Well George done his two-year stretch and worked

in the fields and learned to carpenter pretty good and to bake some and what he really liked was the electric shop, by the time he left he could wind a squirrel-cage electric motor or shunt. And he could solder real good, not just wires but pipe wiring which damn few know how to do any more but it is good to know, and sheet metal joining, lapped or formed. Also auto shop. Also he was pretty good with math, by the time he left he had enough geometry to measure a field or a wall-to-wall carpet and enough trigonometry to figure the angles for a timber truck-ramp and enough algebra to last him the rest of his life, he didn't like it or English. He did not play ball but he liked to root for his building. Any job he could do by himself he liked best. He did not like to hold one end while someone held the other. From General Science the Physics part he got the word Resultant. Put down a weight and drop a rope against it, and you pull one end north and I pull the other end west, the weight will not move north and it will not move west but it will move in a resultant direction northwest. Now when George pulled north he liked the load to go north, not anything different. So whatever other people called cooperation George called Resultant and it made him uneasy until he could do it alone.

Almost two years and no hunting and that was a funny thing because after they let you out of the Cage—that was the big building with the barbwire they took you to first—you were not tied down. You had to be where they told you when they said, and that was most of the time, but there was woods across the fields to the south and if you wanted to slip away maybe and hunt a little you could. George just did not seem to want it. Well they kept you busy and there was never enough time to do all the things around the buildings you wanted to do. Hunting, he just never thought of it.

But then right at the end of the second year they called him to the office and he said to himself well this is it, I'm sprung. But that was not what they wanted to tell him. They said they were sorry about the news but his father was dead. He just stood there in the office and stared at them, Mrs. Dency the fat matron and Miss Grasheim the big ugly nurse although she was nice, and one of the typists who you could see was horning in to see if she could get a charge out of him breaking up or something. Well she had to do without as he kept standing there sort of blinking and trying to percolate the idea all the way in until finally Mrs. Dency said, "I'll tell you what, George, I'll phone your building and tell them to let you upstairs. Perhaps you'd like to lie down and think it over for a while." Which was just exactly one hundred percent what he wanted just then. Which was the good thing about that fat Mrs. Dency, about eight times out of ten she could hit it right on the nose, whatever you needed. As he walked away she told him he could come talk to her whenever he felt like it. When he got to his building she had phoned ahead so he went right up, which during the day was not allowed, and fell down on his bed. He was supposed to be thinking things over but for a time there he could not think of anything to think. When something finally came it was like a weak joke —well, if you're going to live at an orphange you might as well be one.

He got up after a while and took off his shirt and loosened his belt and pushed the front of his pants down below his belly button and stuck his stomach out over the buckle. He stood looking down at the stomach for a while and then shook his head and fixed himself up again. What he thought about just then was not the father squirting blood out of the mother's nose or hollering drunk coming down the cowpath or standing like lost in the courtroom while they sent him up. It was his face the time George stole that first bag of groceries, his face altogether with broken veins in the skin and mottled patches and the dirty-white blonde eyebrows and hair and the two red scoops of his lower lids and his little washed out pink and blue eyes and all the snaggly stinking teeth—the whole nothing mess of a face with all the messy nothing parts, put together for just once, for just one lousy second, in a way that pleased George to think of, surprised and proud, saying he'd amount to something.

George shook himself hard and lay down on the bed. He did not feel anything special, not even relieved. Well his father had not been any kind of a weight on him to feel good taken off.

So finally because of that it came to him what he was supposed to be thinking about. He never did have no real plans, just overall to learn a trade and be able to get a job some place, but he never thought before the some place could be some other place than that one mining town or live in any other house but that shack on the cowpath. The father would be there and that is why he would go there. Now the father would not be there.

So all of a sudden it hit him. Not hit him, it was not like a blow at all. Like one time when he was a little kid he was over to the river and he lay down in an old rowboat tied to some willows and drowsed in the sun. And lying there he watched the grain of the dry gray wood where once was a knot, and the way the deep furrows of the weathered wood swirled in and around and out of that knot, you see things like that sometimes that though they do not move your eye keeps going into and out of and around and back again there are two spirals of hair on a cat's back that way. Anyway he watched that for a long time until he got to know it well and half asleep and he also got to know the feel of the side of the boat on his head and the bottom of the boat on his back and rump. And something made him sit up suddenly and there wasn't anything around him he had ever in his life seen before. The boat had slipped the rope and drifted down the current a half mile or more. But what tore him like a big pair of hands one pulling up one down was how strange it was out of the boat plus how familiar it was inside the boat. He could not move for a long time except to look out at the strange banks and look down into the selfsame knothole over and over again and feel that selfsame gray board grinding his hip. It was like he could take all new or all old not both.

George felt lost and ripped like that on his bed thinking about the father dead. Because here in the school was the most real living he ever done if living is going ahead into newer and newer things. It was here and now and real, but everything out there was all different and like it had never been what he thought it was last time he looked.

He got up off the bed and looked out the window. It wasn't but about four o'clock, a late spring day, and he had no place to be now till 6:30 anyway and even if he did not show then Mrs. Dency would not say nothing, not today.

Even if it was all right something made him be careful, he stopped halfway down the stairs to let two guys walk by down there and get out of sight, and then instead of striking off across the fields he went to the hay barn and through it and down that way.

Once he was in the woods he felt better right away. Up here it was mostly oak and maple and he missed the ragged skinny birches and without the jack pine it smelled way different. But the leaves were all new and not growed yet. Right away he seen a red squirrel but he did not do anything about it, a gray squirrel he might but never a red, they can about jump over a bullet and duck down and peek up at the underside before its gone by. But he saw droppings on the new grass and just when he thought woodchuck he saw the torn maple leaves on a new sprout so it was hedgehog and he cussed, he couldn't catch up with old Porky without he had gloves and a knife which he had not, no knives in that place. The red squirrel paced him in the trees overhead yammering loudern two jaybirds and a dry axle.

Suddenly George fell down and lay still but he had the right cocked way back as he lay on his left side. He never tried this before but it was in a book about a gray fox in the library.

The squirrel spooked out to the outside hair of a maple where there wasn't nothing but two leaves and a breeze to hold him but he was held up somehow, and all the time chit-chitting and scolding and quarreling fit to drive everything from ants to elk three quarter miles. George never moved. The squirrel liked no part of that. He never seen this before and seem like he did not think it was right. He scampered back to the tree trunk and down and out again lower down and took to hissing and squeaking and clacking his teeth together even, but George never moved. The squirrel ran back to the trunk and flaked off a couple scales of bark with his teeth and brought them back and dropped them one by one on George, one hit him right on the cheek and eye, and he never moved. The squirrel cussed up a storm and ran back to the trunk and right down on the ground and stood there on three legs with one front paw on the trunk ready to scoot back up in case, but George never moved. The squirrel grounded the fourth paw and shut up a minute and still George lay there. The squirrel came forward the way a squirrel and specially a red squirrel never does, not jumping but squiggling along on his claws with his legs stiff and his tail straight out behind and for eight, nine inches or so he looked like he was on little wheels and then he hit dry leaves that rustled and scared him and he disappeared like in a trick movie and there was his head peeking around the tree trunk. And now when George did not move the squirrel came out in two big bounds and stopped a yard away and began giving him hell again, and made one small jump closer and George lashed down with that cocked right just in that split second while the squirrel was in the air in the one small jump; if the little redhead saw it coming which he certainly did there was not a thing he could do about it. George's fist slammed him down so hard if the squirrel wasn't there the fist would of gone into the ground up to the wrist but instead he killed that squirrel altogether flattening ribs and all between them against the ground. After that George felt lots better.

He stayed in the woods for another hour but did not see nothing but a brindle bat asleep upside down under an aspen crotch and who wants to bother with bats. He would of liked a large jackrabbit or a young possum but this woods seemed to be fresh out, anyway the squirrel had done his bit and that was a heck of a whole lot better than nothing.

After supper he went to see Mrs. Dency. She put him in a connie and went for some papers and then came back with them and closed the door. "Sit down, George," she said because he had learned to stand up and wait.

"Thank you ma'am," he said because he had learned to say Thank you and Ma'am both.

"Feel better? Yes, I see you do. George, I'm *awfully* sorry."

"It's all right," George said.

She leaned back and pursed up her mouth the way she always wrapped small surprises. She had black hair with a patch of white on one side in front and round black-rimmed glasses with a snivvy fixed to them where they went behind the ears with a cord on so if they dropped off they would just hang. George said, "I always figured to go back but now I don't care."

Mrs. Dency unpursed the mouth and smiled. "How—about—your *aunt?*" She handed over the idea like it was a chocolate-covered thousand dollar bill. The smile went away because George just sat there. "Wouldn't you like that, George?"

George said No.

Now this aunt, the mother's sister, had put in for George a couple times before. The two sisters never did get along and Aunt Mary was the oldest and was real mad that George's mother got married first and things like that. Then when the father took to drinking and things got bad and she found out, she would ask to take George every once in a while but just to put on the dog or rub George's mother's nose in it, but not that she wanted George. Then she married this two-bit hillside farmer in Virginia and more than ever the best way she could think of to put her sister down was to ask for George because it was a way of saying he would be better off with her, which was a way of saying she was better off. Now that the mother was dead George did not trust this offer one bit because he could not see no reason for it. Also George did not get along with Aunt Mary's husband the little he had seen of him. Also George knew the both of them would hold it against him he got sent up for breaking and entering and attempted burglary, and never let him forget it. But George did not say any of this because he never did say much of anything and besides he thought it was his business, he just said No.

Mrs. Dency talked it around a whole lot and the upshot was George just asked to stay right where he was. This was a big surprise to Mrs. Dency but she thought it over and then said okay, because George was only fifteen then and his two years was up but in another year he would be sixteen and the school could turn him loose without he had to go to no relative.

George was wrong on a couple of counts here but he never found that out until later, how could he if he would not talk it over but just sat there.

So he stayed at the school for one more year and you would not know there was any difference, he worked in school and in the auto shop and in the fields and rooted for the ball team and his building won a corn shuck and George won the only thing he ever won in any kind of a race, it was eating blueberry pie with your hands tied behind your back.

But there was a difference all the same. The two years, that is what the court said and the court and the school had a hold on George. If he went over the wall they would of dragged him back and it would be the cage for him and no movies or ice cream till hell froze over. But in this other year, he done his stretch already and he was there because there was not no place he would rather go to although he never said that, they would have macerated him. He never did think serious of going over the wall but if he did it would not be like capturing a escaped criminal it would depend on this and that and the other thing like was he in any more trouble and did he have a clean place to live and all that, and if he was not in no trouble they would of left him alone without even bringing him back. And somehow this all made a big difference to George and it was not a good difference, it was worse.

He was smart enough not to let it show but a thing like that is all in the way you feel. The only thing he did different from before was he slipped out into the woods all the time. He never took nobody with him and he did not do much except once a whole litter of foxes and that was practically an accident. Otherwise it was not too much good because you do not club rabbits without you can get to a meadow edge in the dark to wait for sunup and you do not like to set a real big deadfall or a figure-four without you are sure you can leave it where no one can come and also get to it whenever you want to. It was nice getting away every once in a while but on the other hand it was never enough and it was never right. Like if you want something real real bad it is better if you do not get none at all than if they keep feeding you a little tiny bit all the time.

But the big mystery to George is how come he

could go two whole years without even thinking about the woods and all of a sudden for a year he missed it so much there was a hot place in his belly for it all the time. And the two years went by like nothing but the number three was like forever with its feet dragging.

About the end of it, George got a message to go see Mrs. Dency and he did, and she took him in her office and closed the door and there stood Aunt Mary herself. She was a little woman and George always knowed that but not as little as this, probably because he got so big in the meantime. She looked like the mother but not much. She had a very long nose that was always red at the tip and he thought wet under that, and when she talked she had one of those soft voices like pigeons or something so she could tell you what time it was and make it sound good. George knew the minute he seen her he was not mad at her if he had ever been. She should of come the year before, it would of been the same. But how can you know something like that?

Mrs. Dency like had it all thought out what she would say and what Aunt Mary should say and you can bet she had Aunt Mary in that office a whole hour before, to tell her just how to handle George. So once George was in and he and Aunt Mary said hello and all, and the women sat down and George said, thank you ma'am no thanks and just stood there, Mrs. Dency took a deep breath and started in at the far edge and come around and around what she was trying to say, while Aunt Mary sat straight up on the front rail of the wicker-seat chair looking bright-eyed like a dog when you got meat in your hand and he thinks it is for him but is afraid to say so yet. So in a way it was funny when finally Mrs. Dency got around to saying Aunt Mary still wanted George to come live at the farm, you could see she was like going to touch it and then bounce way off and come in again slow, but George said, and it was the first peep out of him since the hello, he said, "Why sure I will."

Mrs. Dency could not no more stop than if she had fell off a cliff and was halfway down, she went on for almost a minute explaining all about blood is thicker than water and the advantages of a home and family and the only thing stopped her was Aunt Mary got up and came over to George and took hold of both his hands. So that settled that.

It was a long ride on the bus and Aunt Mary did not talk too much and George like always talked hardly at all but by the time they got to the farm George understood a lot of things, one was that nobody held it against him he got sent up because when you get right down to it he did not get sent up for no breaking and entering and attempted burglary, at least not no two years worth, it was mainly because the court and the priest and the welfare woman figured he would be better off at the school than in a shack with the town drunk after the mother died. Also that maybe after all she wanted him to come just because she wanted him to come and not to spite nobody like the mother always used to say. So the only thing to worry about was her husband, a tarheel name of Grallus, Jim Grallus, Uncle Jim. At first sight he was not nothing to worry about being only five four and skinny but like a lot of little guys, he had a mad at all big guys especially when he could tell them what to do, you run across that all the damn time in the army. But even when he was sixteen years old George knew about that and like everything else it is not so bad if you expect it. And anyway it did not show very much on Uncle Jim not for a very long time anyway.

Living on the farm at first was hard on George it was so different from the school, for one thing they gave him a room all to himself and that was much better but for the longest time he could not get used to more than three walls around his bed, it was like your mouth was taped up and half your nose, you could breathe all right but never enough. But in time George got to like the room to himself real good. Also there was always this about George, put him in a new place with new people and he clammed up even more than usual and for a long time he could see Aunt Mary and Uncle Jim thought he was simple, just Yes and No and All right and when they said to tell them something like how was it at the school or back home, just sort of smile and spread out your hands and don't say nothing.

So for the first part of the time, eight, nine months, while George was like settling in, he had to go into the woods a whole lot and long as he done his work which he did, they let him. There was real good woods around there better even than Kentucky, he even seen bears a couple of times although he never did get one. But you never seen such possum, big and fat, and coons and rabbits and even beaver but not much. So at first George went hunting because somehow he had to and then he went just to keep making sure he could and then he met Anna and cut it out altogether, why it was like the first two years at the school, he did not even think of it no more.

He was past sixteen when he met Anna and she was older maybe eight years. Her old man had close to two hundred acres where Aunt Mary had but 46 and that mostly clay pasture, rocks and wood hillside. Anna's pa's place was worse even, and seven kids. George always thought how nice that must be, all those folks like belong to each other, here he was with nobody to talk to. But talking to Anna he found out how she used to think all the time, how nice it must be for him, a small place, so quiet, only thirteen head to milk night and morning, and a room of your own. It was really funny how they envied each other.

George met Anna at the creamery one time when

her pa was laid up with a wrenched shoulder falling off a hay tedder. She drove a team to the creamery and he helped her get the forty-quart cans off the buckboard on to the stage. They did not talk very much at first, she was not what you would call good looking which is why she was stuck so long on that farm, nobody was about to marry her. She had a wide pink face and brown eyes and hair, and carried her head sort of forward the way women do who have that lump up between their shoulders they call the widow's hump. She was big around the upper arms and thighs both but very small in the waist and forearms and ankles and feet. Somehow a woman built like that did not get George all excited but it made him feel comfortable.

He said to her about the third time he saw her that it was close to twelve miles by road from Aunt Mary's around to her pa's place, but did she know it was not more than a mile and a half through the woods. She thought about it and gave him a smile and said yes that's so, and it was because the two farms was around the mountain shoulder from each other, and the roads followed the valleys. Well he said maybe some time he was out hunting he would see her in the fields. She said maybe and that was all just then because the next time he went to the creamery it was her pa. He never did talk to her pa.

So not long after, it was in the summer time and light for a couple hours after milking, sure enough he went out into the woods and struck off up the mountain and down again and before you know it there he was.

And she was sitting outside the barb wire at the edge of the woods by her pa's north pasture.

And he said, What are you doing sitting out here?

And she laughed and said, I reckon I was waiting for you.

And that was the beginning of it, how they used to have long talks about how lucky she was with all that big family, how lucky he was without no family, and all that. He never was with a girl before but she knew a lot, but always careful, fellows working through with the threshing machine and like that, that did not live around those parts. You might think that would make George mad to find out about that but he did not mind. Those fellows was all part of the past and that was gone, she did not have no steady fellow then but she did now and it was him. She showed him what to do pretty much. You would not believe it but George never pushed her to do it. They done all what she wanted to do and he was glad to do it, but it was for her. It was always for her, the way she wanted it. He was always afraid he would hurt her hands or something. It was not until maybe the third week he kind of took over. A warm night and more than anything she smelled good to him. She smelled good the way a cow's breath smells good, the way cut hay smells good, or the milkshed on a warm morning before any spills get to souring. He got that burning in his stomach like when he needed to hunt, but that was always part angry and this was not angry at all. She told him no at first, this wasn't right, but he kept on, and soon she just let him. Well, she knew he would never hurt her and also that he would never talk about it.

That was the best time of George's whole life, better than the army or the school or anything else. Sometimes Uncle Jim was real rough on him depending on how he felt, and sometimes George would do something wrong, just not knowing any better, like the time he built a haystack so it fell over and the time he let the chickens run in the old shed where they got the coccydiosis or however you spell it, the first day they droop, the second day they can't walk, the third day they're dead, it's a wonder they didn't lose the whole flock. George did not like to make mistakes, it made him feel bad and mad at himself. If only Uncle Jim could understand that but he could not. He had to yammer and yell. And sometimes it was bitter cold and sometimes hot and sometimes he had to work two days and nights without stopping like when the calf got born crosswise the same time the windstorm took out more than half the fencing. And his axe jumped off a knot one time and sliced right down through the side of his shoe and into his foot. But with all the trouble and arguments and hard work and all, it was still the best time of his whole life. Nothing ever happened to set him out roaming the woods again with a club or a trap, he just did not need it. He went out a whole lot and they thought it was to hunt, but it was to see Anna. Even not seeing her sometimes was wonderful, like letting yourself go hungry on purpose to make the next meal taste better, which you can do if you are awful sure of the next meal. Anna liked it too, nobody paid her much mind around her place long as she carried her chores. Which she did.

And the funny thing was nobody ever found out, and George and Anna never much tried to keep it a secret. It got like a habit, that's all, for them to meet all alone in the woods and a kind of cave they knew about. Sometimes they saw each other at the grange or in town and talked, but everybody knew everybody and no one thought anything of it. And the way people like to talk, to do matchmaking and all, they still never thought anything about George and Anna. He was only fifteen when he come there first, and she twenty-four or so, and he was big and good looking enough that some of the girls in town used to kid him and yell at him and all, and Anna was one of those people who are in crowds, you know they are there but you can't see their face. So even when folks saw them together in town nobody thought anything of it and nobody ever saw them anywhere else. George he was too young to think about marrying and besides he had no money, and Anna she probably never even thought about it, there are some people who say to theirselves, well, I guess that is not for me, not ever, and they never think about it again, well, Anna had passed that long ago. Two and a half years that way, and you know it is, you think whatever it is you are doing is just naturally going to go on forever. Well it ain't.

There was a time when George and Uncle Jim Grallus had a real bad blowoff, it was in November and it got dark early, and after milking and supper George slipped off in the woods and went over the hill and him and Anna spent a long time fixing up the kind of cave they had up there near her pa's north pasture. It was not much but it was out of the wind. Well what with the work and then fooling around with Anna it was pretty late when he got back.

He did not find out until much later what it was happened while he was gone, but there was something stealing chickens every night or so and it must be Uncle Jim heard them worrying in the middle of the night or something, anyway out he come in his pajamas and a lantern. There was this big skunk outside the chicken run, when it seen him it went into the harness room under the barn. Uncle Jim was mad at that skunk and he took off after it and with his lantern he could see it scrunched up in the corner looking at him. There was a hay fork there and he was so mad he snatched up the hay fork and lunged at the skunk, well one of the tines went through the skin on the skunk's side and stuck into the wall, and there it was caught and there was uncle Jim caught too because everyone knows about a skunk how it smells, but nobody ever seems to mention it has pretty fair claws and a face full of teeth as sharp as a cat and as quick and strong as a wolf. And this was a big one. So Uncle Jim could not turn loose the fork and the skunk could not get loose either, it must have went crazy. Well Uncle Jim hollered a lot but what with being round the other side of the barn from the house, and the wind—it was one of those cold fall nights with a half a moon and a half a gale—Aunt Mary did not hear. And George was not even there but Uncle Jim did not know that.

Well he yelled his self hoarse and he was cold to boot, and how he stunk too. Maybe he thought to let the skunk bleed to death but it was not bleeding much so he just leaned on the fork and kind of dozed. And woke up and shivered and dozed.

So about this time George come back. In the moonlight he seen the back barn door open, but no light because the lantern had long gone out. So George he just walked that way instead of straight past. He bumped the door shut and dropped the bar and went on into the house. The sound of the bar just naturally snapped Uncle Jim out of it and he hollered and jumped for the door but by then George turned the corner and with the wind in his ears and thinking, I guess about Anna, he did not hear nothing. So there was Uncle Jim in the pitch black with the skunk and when he jumped for the door he dropped his fork. They went round and round in there a whole lot. In about ten minutes the noise fretted the big Holstein bull, well, mostly Holstein, that was in stanchions on the main floor of the barn, the bull got to tossing against the stanchions, the cows got restless, it woke the hogs, maybe the sow lay over on a shoat, but anyway the shoat started to squeal. By this time there was noise enough for George Smith to hear and George Washington to boot. George run out there and was all over the yard and barn before he finally heard the cussing and banging from the harness room. He run down there and opened up and the first thing comes out is smell, like a wall falling on you, like something solid. Then the skunk so mad it could not touch the ground, it just flew and they never did get that skunk, George he just blinked and let it go by. Then come Uncle Jim.

And all he wanted to know was who shut the door

and dropped the bar on him. And George said he did but.

But nothing. Then and there Uncle Jim started in and he cussed George out up and back and down again. If George had anything to say Uncle Jim did not want to hear it, he got through all he could think of about George is stupid and clumsy and lazy and if he thinks he is wise well he has another think coming. And the more he yelled the madder he got, it was like he had a pot full of hate for George and everything about George with the lid screwed down tight and the lid blew off and everything exploded out. Maybe if George was as handy with his mouth as some guys it would not have been so bad, but all he could do was stand there like a dummy and every once in a while, smile. This was not really a smile, he sure did not feel like smiling, but it come out like that. It seemed to put Uncle Jim crazy. He started in on a whole new line of stuff, like he brung up another layer. He said about George's mother and father they were never married, George was a bastard. He said about George he was a queer, what he meant was I guess George did not have a girl that he knew about, just liked to go off by himself in the woods. He said George's father was a no good drunk and his mother would of been a whore if she was not too goddam ugly and George was a robber and a burglar and a jailbird and he was sick and tired of his face around.

George still did not feel like smiling but he could not think of nothing to say so he smiled. Uncle Jim begun to yell even more, it started to be words, but spit was coming out of his mouth and like sudsing up, his eyes was real crazy, one of them cocked to one side. He started to hit George. He was so little and George was so big he had to reach up to get to his face. George had fists half the size of Uncle Jim's head, and he never even put them up. George had a sheath knife on his belt and he never even thought about it. Uncle Jim hit and hit at him, he was not strong enough to finish it with any punch but just kept cutting. George like pushed at him a little and backed away but the screaming, the way the suds kept flying off Uncle Jim's mouth, it kept him lost. He felt blood on his mouth and tasted it. He hollered, just a great big whoop of a holler, and run away. Uncle just stood there yelling And dont come back And dont come back.

George did not rightly know where he was going, he really did not know which way he was headed until he was in the sort of cave him and Anna had fixed up. He crawled in there, he was breathing hard like running or crying and blood dripping off him and water in his eyes, he smelt all over the old blanket they had in there and lay down and rolled back and forth. He needed something real bad he did not know what. Mostly it was Anna but Anna was by now in bed asleep and no way to get to her without making trouble for everybody. Now if he could of gone to Aunt Mary maybe she could of helped but there was no way of doing that without being next to Uncle Jim. And he thought about Mrs. Dency but she was miles away, he would never see her again. His stomach was hot and his face and head hurt. In the moonlight he could look down and see the blood drip down from his chin to his hand, it looked black, he thought it was his mother's blood.

He hollered out again like he did down by the barn. Then he sat still for a long time not even thinking. Then he got up and cut out through the woods, heading along the north fence of Anna's pa's place and away at the corner and downhill through the woods to the road. On the way he stopped at the brook and cleaned up. It was very cold. He did not care about that, it felt good. He went to town.

He cut off the road near town and come to it through woods like he liked to. There was a factory there where they made paper boxes and kraft bags out of yellow pine that grows like a weed on worked-out cotton land. There was a railroad siding. There was a little shack there with a watchman. That there watchman had George's father's face. That watchman was drunk, he smelled of sweet and dirty skin and cheap liquor just like the father, he yelled at George sudden the same old way, like he did not have to draw breath, it was there ready for yelling.

That whole thing was too much for George and so he slid back into the woods and he roamed around in there for a long time, three, four days. He never did remember. He did not eat sleep probably not even a drink of water. One thing came clear later like a picture, it was the cave and the smell of their blanket and Anna sitting by him crying. Whatever else really happened is only what he was told. Anna brought him back to Aunt Mary's place. He was weak and sick and he had a bad fever, and how she took him so far is a miracle but then she was pretty strong.

He was sick a week, just laying there in his room and not saying nothing even when he got well enough to. Aunt Mary explained about Uncle Jim as much as she could, especially when he was not around to hear her. She said he was a little man through and through and always was mad at a big man just for that. She even told him they had quarreled, her and Uncle Jim, about George. He never really said there was funny business but he said she looked at big old George with his yellow hair and his muscles in a way that she should not even if she did not know it herself. And also Uncle Jim was no spring chicken no more. So when you added it up it was a high heap, Uncle Jim was mad at him because he was young, because women thought he was good looking, because he was strong, because his wife liked him, and on top of all that because he could not figure him out, you can not when a guy never says anything. So to cream it off on the top is, Uncle Jim thought that night with the skunk he was laughing at him. George was not laughing at him. A thing like that is funny but not when you are there.

Uncle Jim never said he was sorry or anything but Aunt Mary said he was and George believed her. Uncle Jim just never mentioned it again and you would not believe it but things went on like before. But you have to remember George was used to all hell breaking loose and then everything just going on again, from he was a child. Maybe things was even a little better than before. Uncle Jim, he had shot himself a big lump and it was slow to fill up again, also he must be trying to hold off from that type thing he was not proud of. It did not really make much difference to George, he was used to it, and Aunt Mary was as kind as she could be while scared of what Uncle Jim said about liking George too much. But it really was better and no fooling with George and Anna, because it done Anna a lot of good to take care of him that once when he could not help himself, and it done George good too. There was many a time when George thought back to that, cuts and fever and the whole thing, it was what a guy really wants all the way down inside—to have your fill, to be safe with someone taking care, and just to quit thinking.

Everything smoothed over like that until George was nineteen and Anna got sick.

The only good thing about it was George knew why she was sick, she was knocked up, that is why. If she just did not show up and he got to hanging around her pa's place asking, it would of been even worse a mess. Because he was never sure but he thought they knew what was wrong with her and you can bet they were crazy trying to figure out who was the guy. They was a stiff-neck bunch, her folks, and they would not let it get around but all the same, any guy around asking after her would of been on the spot. So it was a good thing he knew and could stay away. She was sick already when she told him. She was throwing up all the time, they call it morning sickness but this did not need mornings, she could not hold nothing on her stomach any time. She missed her period two times already, well, he knew that really before she did, she never used to keep track. So when she stopped showing up after chores it was because she had to stay in bed sick. That was only a nuisance at first but when it got to be two weeks, four and six and seven, it was hard to take. George had grew to need Anna, he could not get along very easy without he saw her. And he begun to worry either she was so sick she would not get better and then what would he do? or she was getting better or was even better already but she was mad and not taking no more chances with him. Either one of these ideas he could not stand and he hopped from one to the other all the time. And he had to admit in spite of these years he was seeing her he really did not know her well enough to know if she would dump him over such a thing as that.

What he did besides worry was to hate that little bugger inside her. Even if it was only a baby or less that made it worse. There it was warm and fed all the time with nothing to do or even think about while George had to do without. Like if Anna had some other fellow and George had to lose out to another guy that was stronger or smarter or richer or something, well he might be sore and sad too but at least the guy who beat him out was something, was more some ways than George. But this animal in her, growing like some sort of big wart or something inside her, it was a real nothing, but it beat him out hands down without even trying, without even knowing he was there. And it was the only thing he ever got mad at her for, what did she want to get herself knocked up for, he could have done without that, it was just her wanted it and now look.

He used to see to his traps, he went back to hunting

again a whole lot, and then he would go to the cave and set there and whittle with his sheath knife and the only thing he did was hating that thing inside of her.

Which is how he come to join the army, because things got so bad he could not sleep or nothing, he had that hot in his stomach almost all the time and it was harder and hard to get rid of. It was like word got around in the woods, everything gone from there, rabbits, coons, chucks, even chipmunk and mice, and what was left was skinny and runty. But he was kidding himself. One time with the biggest fattest possum he ever did see he felt the same way.

Still he took to looping out wider and wider, he did not know what he was looking for but just thought he might find it somewhere else if he could not find it around home. And it was in the middle of the summer he found a beaver lodge way up the hills and went to work on a deadfall, it would have to be a big one because beaver is hard to hold. And he always always set traps where nobody ever went, this was not to save anybody any trouble, it was just no sense at all to set traps where people was slamming around yelling and jabbering. There is not one man in eight hundred dozen knows how to be quiet anywhere, let alone woods, that is what is mostly wrong with people. So anyway he come back the next day to this deadfall by the beaver lodge and here was a damn little snotnose kid caught up by the leg. Well this made George so damn mad it is funny but so damn mad he felt better. You get that mad when you are all like lost and mixed up, you do not feel lost any more at least while you are mad. He clobbered that kid good for tripping the deadfall, the kid was for him the kid growing in Anna and pushing him out of the way, he could hit out at the kid at last.

The next day he went to town and saw the man at the post office and the first thing Aunt Mary knew about it was when he brought back the papers for her to sign, he was on his way. It come so sudden she and Uncle Jim did not know what to say even, she kind of puddled up and Uncle Jim just kept on saying Well whaddaye know, well whaddaye know, and when George was in his store clothes he said Son all we did was the best we could. George he just smiled that smile he had when he did not know what to say, and he took off.

Well they say a lot about the army it is no good, it is hurry up and wait, it is this lousy army, this goddam army. Well I am here to tell you there is lots of guys get a better deal in the army they ever got before, there is a lot of them griping the worst never had a word to say before they got the wrinkles out of their belly the first time in their whole lives. There is better grub than army grub but army grub is a whole lot better than a lot of these guys ever saw before at least that regular. And you would be surprised how many guys never in their whole life got enough sleep week in week out and kept themselves clean before. You do what they tell you and never volunteer, and you find you got a life. You want to worry, go ahead, but it will be all peanuts and chicken spit you are worrying about, the big things is all thought out for you, you do not have to worry yourself. I said this before and I will have to say it again, when you come right down to it there is not a thing a man needs than a way to fill his belly and let somebody take care of all his thinking, he don't have to if he don't want to. And if that is not the army through and through I do not know what is.

For once in his life George figured he done the right thing. He was sorry sometimes he could not see Anna but whatever happened to her she was not alone in the world and she would be all right unless she died and then what can you do. Anyway for the two-year hitch and training and motor mechanic school George had everything he wanted and for once some money besides. It was the state school all over again for him only bigger and easier too. When he come to the school he had to spend a long time learning what to do and what not, but in the army he already knew, he knew better than a lot of guys who never lived in a dormitory or a barracks before. He did not bother with nobody and nobody bothered with him, he was still a big guy who kept his mouth shut which is the recipe for getting left alone if you want to.

Time come to re-enlist he did, you know he did not even take his furlough but just hung around the base, it was in California. And it could be he fell in this slot people are always falling in, getting the idea that things are going to go on like they are for ever. Well they aint.

First a lot of rumors and you know how to shuck off rumors, but what really happened was one of the rumors you shucked off. The whole outfit shipped overseas. Some said it was a war and some a police action and I guess it was a big joke to some of them.

For George it was bad, there was nobody to talk to about it and he would not know what to say if he did. He moved around a lot in the army, Louisiana, New Jersey, Michigan, California, but no move was like this move. And that old hot place come back to him in his gut, and there was not much he could do about it. Overseas it was not so easy to go off hunting and there was not much to hunt if you did. And there was none of this trading passes and easy coming and going. Every thing was laced up a notch, tight.

Then there was drilling and that never bothered George, but this one day it was on the airstrip and these three C-119s came in with casualties and they told off infantrymen for stretcher-bearers. They took out one hundred and sixty three stretcher cases altogether and you see this and you hear this and you are never the same again.

All you can say about the way George felt is he

was a little kid again he was going to get for something he did or for nothing. The father would do it but the father coming home, even coming home drunk, did not mean he would get hit just then. The only thing you could be sure of was getting hit, that was going to happen and no fooling. You just never knew when, that is all. And George with the school and the farm, but especially the army, George had like grown away from all that, it was dead and gone and past so forget it. And then these casualties, they were for real. So getting hit for sure, but you don't know just when—here it was again. And here it always had been. George thought he left it behind, well he did not. And maybe tonight and maybe next week you would go over there where they made stretcher cases out of men. And when you went maybe you would not get yours tonight or next week, but get it you pos-i-loot-ly would.

George was not the only one felt this way and he knew it. Some laughed and talked louder and ran faster and did everything heavier and some slunk off every chance they got and sat and looked worried, and some spent all their time figuring out how to get loose just one time and get especially drunk. But George, there was only one thing he wanted and needed and he began to think of Anna, think of Anna like he never did before, think of Anna so much he could almost smell Anna the way she was, warm.

And there was not nothing he could do about it, that was the worst. So what he done was as hard as anything he ever did because he never done it before, he decided to write a letter. It must have took him four days to write that letter and most of the time was just sitting looking at the paper. Then he wrote his letter and that was that, it did not make him feel no better but it was all he could think of to do and he done it and there was nothing more he could do. And nobody else knew how he felt. He never was a talker. When somebody talked to him about getting shipped over, he would just smile. I guess nobody really knew at all.

Then one day they called him to see this doctor, this colonel. And he went and that is where I began this story. Phil said I could begin it any place as long as I explained whatever I said.

Well old George Smith just went stateside and he clammed up like he never did in his life before, and when you come down to it it is a good idea nobody bothered with him once they welded him into that tank. Because he was away down deep crazy mad at first. Not crazy, crazy mad, there is a big difference. So anyone pushing at him when he felt that way he would of just got stubborn maybe fight some more. But a crazy mad is like a fire, you shut it up by itself for long enough it is just naturally going to go out.

So one day the door opened and the guard let in this doctor, only he was just a sergeant and not very big. Bigger than Uncle Jim but not very big. And he had black bushy hair and glasses and he right away said he was a doctor all right but call him Phil and how did he feel. And George could of broke him in two over his knee or snapped him like a rattlesnake when you want to break his neck you got no stick, but Phil just waved at the guard go away, and the guard locked him in and Phil sat down near him on the bed and handed cigarettes although this George Smith never did smoke he wished he did.

So Phil was smoking and keeping his mouth shut and George Smith begun to feel easier and finally Phil asked him what did he want most of all and George said Out. And Phil asked Why. And George was surprised at this but if it was a stupid question Phil did not look stupid. So George said, To go back to his girl and get married. Because George knew now of all the places in the world he could go to, it would have to be next to Anna, she knew what he was and she liked it too and nobody else ever would. And he did not want the army no more not after those stretcher cases.

Then Phil told him he could get out but he would

have to do just what Phil said. And George Smith, he was ready to climb the wall and hang off the ceiling if Phil said to. I have to say here that I trust Phil. He wants me out, I am sure of that. I also don't think he wants this writing of mine to be nothing but the truth. He has got nothing to sell, not to me or to anybody who reads this. I would not believe that at first but I do now.

So he told me to write the story of my life and I said I did not know how or even where to begin and he said begin anywhere but be sure you explain everything. He said like a movie or a comic where they start out a guy is an old man and go back to what happened earlier if I wanted to. Just as long as I wrote down everything important so he could understand me better. And he told me if there was trouble getting started then write it about somebody else, because he said that is a good way to back off from yourself, you remember better. So after he went I started in, I made up the name George Smith and he is right. I wrote all the rest of that day and from then on I did not do nothing but write as long as there was any light, and he come back two other times but I was not finished.

So this is the story and it is all true and it is all I can remember. I done the best I could. I do not know why I am here or why I was shipped stateside here to this nut factory instead of the can for just hitting an officer. I am not crazy, anyone is who thinks so. All I want is out. I want out of here and I want out of the army, I had enough. All I want is to go back to my girl, we will get married and leave there or maybe fram some place. Or a store.

Here is another of the letters with the letterhead discarded.

Looneybin Lane
Orgonia, Ore.

O-R
Feb 26

Dear Phil, dammit:

With all I've got to do I have been sitting here pulling on my lower lip and wondering what to say to you. I'm going to tell you right at the start that when I first got that bundle of paper from you and determined it wasn't the Sunday *Chronicle* complete with the spring fashions supplement, I was mad as hell. And I suppose I still am. And I began by feeling that "George Smith" should be thrown out of that maniac's motel of yours, and I wound up feeling the same way. But you made me laugh.

Well of course, you stinking psychologist you. Anything you might have said to me I'd've spit in your eye for, after all this time. If I thought about you and "George" at all, I thought no news is good news and you'd finished with it. Then you send me his autobiography with no comment at all, just *nothing*.

So ruefully, it is to laugh. I know what you're up to. You want me to react, i.e., think. Now you know damn well an administrator doesn't have time to think any more than he has time to plow through a testament like this. You also know me well enough to know

I'd leaf through it and get hauled in and then go back and start over and hit every word. And be impressed by the effort that went into it, not excluding your pecking it all out on the typewriter. (What's the matter —haven't you got enough work to do?) (Seriously, Phil, I know you did it instead of sleeping and cut that out: I need you. You're going to kill yourself.)

Now about the biography. I am doubtless much more impressed by the pathetic horror of it than a case-hardened character like you. I am also impressed by this kid's descriptive ability. I don't know how a fourth-grade English teacher would parse some of his sentences (like his description of the weathered knot of wood in the boat's side: ". . . you see things like that sometimes that though they do not move your eye keeps going into and out of and around and back again there are two spirals of hair on a cat's back that way.") but I never failed to get *exactly* what he meant. And aside from the one or two real insights he comes up with, as for example that discussion on sex and the machine-precise, almost delicate distinction he draws between Satisfy and Relieve, I am impressed by the *completeness* of his story. To this jaundiced eye he has left out nothing of significance; his portrait of himself is filled in to a substantial solid and contains no appreciable holes. What he has left out, like the exact details of his sex techniques with Anna, shouldn't bother anyone except a grubby clinician like yourself who is beyond the reach of the chivalrous asterisk.

I think there are a great many folks on the loose, people who would pass anyone's sanity standards with flying colors, who are *in themselves* a lot sicker than this boy. He's one of the few human beings I've ever heard of who seems to have placed sex in a genuinely wholesome perspective. He's inordinately self-reliant; as long as he's alone, he could no more be lost than a cat can be lost. And that brings up what to my mind is the real nature of his sickness, if any. *And it isn't his sickness.*

I said above that many certifiably sane people are in themselves sicker than "George." Where we can raise an eyebrow at George is in matters which concern, not a person, but people. No human being, not even George, lives entirely alone. Interpersonal flux isn't just fun, or convenient, or decent, or orthodox. It is essential, vital. Homo sap. is an interdependent species. He may *not* live alone. And it's easy to describe how "George" relates to people: he doesn't.

Yet, in him, I don't think it matters. He found Anna. There's an odd aura about that relationship but whatever it is—and I'm not prying—it's suitably convexo-concave, if you see what I mean. She sounds like a girl with pieces missing, but she has the ones he needs.

To sum up I think this guy's only sickness is scar tissue from a regrettable childhood, and his only real crime is in being a loner. It feels criminal to us gregarious souls because we don't think we could do it. It's —well, unfashionable. It makes us uneasy because of an in-the-cells certainty we all have that without our fellows we could not survive. In a herd-and-hive culture like ours, a solitary bent seems in a way immoral. Tsk tsk.

All the foregoing (he said modestly) is of bull-session character; this isn't my specialty, it's yours. For all my irritation, I am grateful to you, old buddy, for a fascinating hour. Now for Christ's sake turn him loose.

as ever,
Al

P.S.: What in *God's* name do you suppose was in that airletter that alerted the major?

Here is the carbon copy of a letter.

Lingam Lane O-R
Catamite, Cal. Feb 28

Dear Kernel, corps of the Nut:

Delighted with your letter, your wisdom, your insight, your perspicacity. You're wrong.

1. There *are* appreciable holes in "George's" narrative, and:

2. His attitude toward sex is not wholesome.

Having said which with such positiveness, I'll have to be honest and say, for item One, that I don't know what the holes are, just where they are. For item Two, I don't think his sexual approach is wholesome but I do not affirm it is unwholesome either. This is not juggling with accepted norms, which are as you know pretty weird in places. It's just that I don't know *what* his sex-matrix is; I'm only sure it will bear investigation.

Like yourself, I've been busy with several thousand other things while all this is going on, and I must remind you that this correspondence, for all these weeks, results just from his voluntary bio and our evaluation of it. I think it's about time I scheduled some real time for him and started digging. I'll let you know what happens. Thanks again for a grand letter.

luv,
Phil

Here is a letter.

Office of the Administrator
Field Hospital HQ
Portland, Oregon

O-R
March 2

Phil:

I'll say this as gently as possible. Friendship, and off-the-record correspondence, as factors *alpha* and *beta*, are desirable as long as they do not interfere with *gamma*, that is, the job. *Alpha* and *beta* are absolutely wonderful where they help with the job. But if *gamma* is injured or slowed, *beta* will have to go and if necessary *alpha*. Because, old buddy, *gamma* is bigger than both of us. I'm using Greek letters because you're an intellectual and I don't want to insult you with ABC's, but Phil, it really is that simple.

I can say I suspect you've been working so hard (and well, I cordially add) that your judgement is wavering. And/or I can suggest that your really admirable preoccupation with your specialty has you chasing subtleties at a time when gross shovelling is piling up on you. This is to your personal credit but no good for the shop. I can even concede that you are right about this patient, but still insist that if he is tilted, it's not enough to roll a marble; shunt him out and forget him. Or if you must, keep track of him and bring him some aspirin when you graduate to being a civilian.

Or, finally, I can say, and you know damn well I will if I have to, that you have to take my orders, Sergeant Outerbridge, even if you know I am wrong. Even if you know I know I'm wrong.

Give me credit for effort literally above and beyond the call of duty, on behalf of the above-mentioned *alpha*. It would cost me to lose it.

Still your friend,
Al

Here is the carbon copy of a letter.

Base Hospital #2
Smithton Township, Cal. O-R
Staff Office March 4

Colonel, suh:

I yield to superior numbers. And eagles. I am as of above date drafting, as ordered, a sound-sounding diagnosis. I'm sorry you had to get stuffy about it, Al. I can see why, but I have to say I'm sorry you did. Oh well. Old Alpha can stand it, I guess.

While I'm sounding (and I'm not dragging my feet on it, sir), here's one thing for you to chew on in your idle moments:

Exactly why did the fully filled-in, admirably portrayed GI blow his stack when asked that specific question by the major?

yrs obediently,
Phil

Here is the answer:

Sime plice O-R
Sime stite. March 13

Phil, you louse:

You have the damndest way of slipping live ants under a man's scalp. Aside from the fact that I have no idle moments, which you know, I made up my mind not to use them on any such dead issue. After four days it bothered me enough that I dug out "Smith's" manuscript to find out exactly what it was the major asked him when he blew his top. It was, and I quote, " 'What do you hunt for, George? I mean, exactly what do you get out of it?' " And then bang.

For two more days I made up my mind, quite often, to forget it. So now, not that it matters, but just for the sake of peace, peace, sweet suffering peace: Mr. Bones, why *did* the nice man blow his stack?

Not that it matters, really. You don't have to answer this.

Al

A carbon copy:

Higgly Hatch
Covercrotch, Cal.

O-R
March 15

I dunno, Al.
Shall I ask him?

Phil

A letter:

Base Hosp HQ
Ptlnd Ore.

O-R
March 16

No!

A. W.

A telegram:

SGT PHILIP OUTERBRIDGE
BASE HOSP # 2
SMITHTON TOWNSHIP CAL MAR 16 6:12 PM

SO ASK HIM.

AL

Another telegram:

SGT PHILIP OUTERBRIDGE
BASE HOSP # 2
SMITHTON TOWNSHIP CAL MAR 16 6:21 PM

HAVE GUARD PRESENT THAT IS AN ORDER
COL ALBERT WILLIAMS

Vultures' Vestry
Luna Park, Cal.

O-R
March 17, begorrah

Dear Al:

I was really touched by your second wire to me last evening. Imagine, it's the first time you actually pulled rank on me and here I am touched.

Actually, your posture of command of recent date so chastened me that I sprang to obey on receipt of your first telegram, and did not get the second, heart-warming one until I came back downstairs.

Work proceeds apace on the clever knowledgeable diagnosis and recommendation for medical discharge, and I imagine we will have it processed in the next few hours, or say 24.

As ever,
Phil

P.S. Oh sure an' you'll be wanting to know phwat the man said. (March 17 always boots me right in the Erse.) He said—and with perfect calm, Colonel: he trusts me, you know, which he will not when (God willing) I get my silver bars, which should be about the time he leaves here. Man, it seems I have been waiting half my life for that commission. Tell me, Al, will I feel as good to get the lowly captain's insignia as you did to get your lofty eagles? . . . but I digress. The man said, when I asked him why he blew up when the major asked him what he got out of hunting small game—you'll remember, he stated in his manuscript that he disapproved of killing for killing's sake, so it wasn't that, and as for the obvious, I don't think he once mentions hunger in connection with hunting; also, he frequently went for periods of months and even years without the slightest desire to hunt; anyway, what he answered was simply that he exploded because he thought the major had found out what it was. When I asked him why that should have bothered him, he explained carefully to me that he never was mad at the major; the major was a nice man; he was mad at himself because he had given himself away. The MP's grabbed him while he was mad, hence the donnybrook. Begorrah. The major pitched in to help and got his nose in the way.

He affirms that if nobody had grabbed him nothing would have happened but his cut hand when he squashed the water glass.

I hope that answers your question, Al. Peace, peace, sweet suffering peace. He'll be a civilian ere the dew drenches the shamrock or shortly thereafter.

P.O.

Base Hospital HQ
Portland, Ore.

O-R
March 19

Dear Phil:

I see what you're up to. To some degree. There's a distinction between absolute and implicit obedience, forever discovered and rediscovered in the ranks and used to bug the officers. For all your light-hearted blarney (you see I'm not immune to the passing of Padraic) you're still bleeding about my pulling rank on you. I can even see how you finagled me into asking just that question (Why did "George" blow his biscuit) when it was perfectly clear I was interested in the same thing the major was: what was his compulsion to hunt, if not for killing nor hunger?

If he's still around by the time you get this, see if you can find out.

And look—just to forestall any of your neurone-prodding, puppet-pulling monkeyshines, let's drop this explicit-answer-to-explicit-question bit. If you get an answer to this question don't go giving it to me with a teaser on it for the next one.

Oh God damn it to hell, Phil. You're bound on this, aren't you? If I don't give you your head with this patient you'll tweeze me to death with your niggling little pokes and pinches. And you know damn well I need you where you are, working as hard as you can, which I gather means working happy. My alternative is to pitch you in the stockade or transfer you out and you know I can't.

Okay, then, go ahead. But give everything you can to everything else. Either get results with him or kick him out.

It's lucky for you we're friends. It's lucky for me you know how to keep your trap shut. As for Nature Boy, I still think you are wrong. Hurry up and prove it.

Al

The Happy Hutch
Far Out, Cal.

O-R
March 21

Dear Al: Bless you, boy! I have everything lined up—Thematic Apperception, Rorschach, projective personality from profile to Patagonia. As for the other work, buddy, you got yourself a dynamo. You have never seen processing like you'll see it now. Thanks thanks thanks and don't ever ask me if I really did start a discharge for "George."

Gratefully,
Phil

Schizoid Center,
Splitconk, Ore.

O-R
March 23

Dear Phil:

Don't thank me, friend; and don't worry, I won't ask you if you really were processing that discharge. You have your dear old Colonel completely submissive and under your thumb, and willing to do anything to assist you. Like I'm holding up your commission until you're quite finished with your authorial playmate, so your being an officer won't upset him. A tough case, Phil, but I'll go along with you if it takes years.

Cordially,
Al

Here's a sheaf of therapy notes, transcribed from shorthand. Q = Therapist. A = Patient. All notes refer to the case termed AX 544.

March 25.
Morning: 3 hours.

Q. Morning, George.
A. Who—me? George? (Lying on cot. Sits.)
Q. (Shrug.) A good name. You picked it.
A. (Nods.) What I wrote. .... It work?
Q. Work?
A. To get me out of here.
Q. It works like a brick, George, building something. Part of a whole lot of things.
A. All that. A brick.
Q. That was two whole truckloads, George. That was a good job.
A. (Lies down. Seems angered. Watches Q, eyes slitted. Respiration slow.)
Q. (Turns back. Walks to window. Fills pipe slowly. Lights. Turns. A. now looking, off-focus, at ceiling.) It takes a lot of bricks. But it's the only way.
A. Okay.
Q. No in-and-out this time, George. I'm here till lunch time. (Pause.) If you want me.
A. (Shrugs slightly.)
Q. Want to get to work, then?
A. Doing what?

Q. What I h[illegible] to do mostly is get to know you real well.
A. Asking questions.
Q. That's one way.
A. Goddam major sent me here . . . he ask too many questions.
Q. (Recognizing warning: don't pry.) Okay. Let's try this, George. (Starts to lay out Wechsler on table. Curious, George gets up.)

The Army Wechsler Mental scale consists of ten types of questions, some requiring good use of language, others, easy mathematical manipulation, still others solving simple picture puzzles. It is a standard intelligence test, not likely to stir up violent reactions.

Q. (More than an hour later, halfway through tests.) You don't talk much, do you, George? What happened: use up all your words writing?
A. (Slipping from passivity to surliness.) Never did talk much. . . . Quit callin' me George.
Q. Okay . . . want me to use your real name? (It is Bela—a natural taunt for American juveniles.)
A. Hell no . . .

(On the Wechsler, he scored at a high average level when it came to understanding conventional meanings and ideas. That is, he knew what was expected of him by people around him. But when the test demanded intense concentration and abstract thinking he did less well. He could not apply his mind to a complex idea or situation. I judged that he was equipped to do it, but was unable—at the moment at least—to use the equipment. It seemed tied up in some other task. He was the figurative clam to the letter, the impenetrable valves open a crack, just sufficient to contact what was immediate, direct, simple, touchable.)

Q. (Looking at watch.) Man, you're *movin!* You know

we're all done with this and we have a whole hour left? You keep on at this rate . . .

A. Yeah? (Drops passivity for a quick look at Q. Searching for sincerity. Unused to praise.)

Q. Want to try more?

A. (Dully.) Okay. (Here one could sense, rather than hear or see, a difference in the dullness. This differed from the genuinely, unstirred phlegmaticism. This was almost identical, but an act to conceal an increased awareness.)

Q. This is called the Rorschach.

A. (Defensively) Shock?

The Rorschach is a set of ten standardized "ink-blots." (You would make such a blot by putting a blob of ink on paper, folding it in two through the blot, pressing the folded paper flat and then opening it up. The blot would be irregular in shape but identical right and left.) To the ten standard Rorschach cards, most people react in certain conventional ways. They see humans or animals or insects or plant life. They see people in traditional poses or action, such as eating, talking, dancing, walking, laughing. These usual reactions are offered spontaneously at sight. There is no "right" or "wrong" way to see Rorschach blots. There is merely approach to or departure from statistical norms.

Q. (Chuckles.) Not "shock." Rorschach. Name of the guy invented them. Just look at 'em one by one and tell me what you see, or what they look like or remind you of.

A. (For the impact second, and for the first time, eyes wide and completely alert. Scansion swift, up, down, across. Then lids lower again to usual hooded attitude; subsequent gaze steady and dull. This particular card usually seen by men his age as two figures dancing around an overgrown tree.) This is like two guys mashing an animal, pulling on it or maybe choking it. It didn't bleed yet but it will. There's the animal's hole. (Pointing to a red spot on the card.)

Q. (Impulsively using a technique applicable to another test entirely.) Why are they doing that?

A. (Instantly withdrawing; concealing; secretive.) They just doing it.

Q. (Another card, oftenest seen as two animals crawling up a hill.) How about this?

A. (Instant response.) That's a tit. Two dragons wanted it but they spoiled it, they tore it all up. Now they are mad, they are flying at it.

Q. Try this. (Usually seen as a large butterfly.)

A. It's like animals pulling apart somebody's body. Vicious animals. There's the girl's spine and her hole. She's cut in half. It's red inside. (Respiration deeper perhaps but slow; eyes hooded; nostrils repeatedly dilated.)

Q. This one?

A. Oh, that's somebody built a double deadfall, bam, it got two animals, chucks maybe or possum, both at once, mashed.

Q. And this?

A. A woman's belly bust open. It was a baby in it bust it. But the baby bust open too, see it there?

Q. (Gathers up the cards. A. watches absorbedly.)

A. (As if he had been thinking about it all this time.) Phil. . . ?

Q. ?

A. You could call me George if you want.

Q. Anything you say. . . . we came a long way today. You're doing real good now. You want to try some more; more kinds, sometime soon? Not now, it's lunch already.

A. (Dully.) Okay.

Q. (Raps for guard.)

End session.

Comments: George has a strange quality about him I call inaccurately non-guilt. It is inaccurate because he is completely aware of good and evil as other people judge them, but he seems burdened not at all by that sense of punishment earned which afflicts most people in a Judo-Christian matrix like ours. An extreme example is the character described from Biblical times right up to the present, who when injured or thrust into misery concludes instantly that this is punishment for a transgression, known or unknown. The cry, "What have I done to deserve this?" seems to mean, "I have done nothing to deserve this!"; actually it means, in many or most cases, "For which of my sins am I being punished?"

In George's case I feel—almost intuitively—that there is in him no conviction of *quid pro quo*, punishment for crime. Punishment he understands, other people's attitudes toward crime he understands. But he simply seems not to share the attitude. A trivial analogy would be two persons, one dedicated to and transported by music, one completely tone-deaf and arhythmic. The latter would recognize that the former was experiencing something, but could not know what it was nor how it felt. George seems in that sense to be "tone-deaf" to a whole spectrum of commonly-shared feelings—empathy for a dying animal, squeamishness in regard to pain, blood, injury, or injustice: a protective coating built up over the years and penetrated apparently only when he saw the casualties. Certainly a great deal of this could be explained by his execrable childhood, where punishment descended without rhyme or reason, while childish breaches of conduct like absence at meals or at night, stealing, impertinence, and disobedience were as often as not overlooked. Punishment did not necessarily follow crime in George's cosmos, yet punishment inevitably came, crime or no.

I have seen a great many prisoners who, for all their griping about a raw deal, actually felt that they were fairly caught and justly punished. A great many felt, or said they felt, that the punishment was too great; few indeed felt that they should not be punished at all. Even some innocent prisoners—innocent, that is, of the crime for which they are convicted—have a notion that they are paying off for *something*. But George's feeling about the long imprisonment which followed his attack on the major was essentially what mine would be if, in crossing a field, my body broke through and fell into an immense labyrinthine cave. I don't think I would feel I deserved it. I would want to find a way out, and if I could not, but met a man there who convinced me he knew the way, I would follow. And if I discovered, as we went along, that it would be not hours nor days, but weeks and even months before we emerged, I think I would feel about the whole thing as George was feeling now.

How could such a creature as George exist for any appreciable time in a modern society? How, if he has so little concept of law and of property, of reciprocity and consequence, could he stay out of trouble for even a day?

It becomes less of a mystery as one thinks it through. George had drifted to either of two environmental poles—the complete license of the outdoors, where laws are impartial and clearly understood, be they laws of gravity or the amount of whip yielded by a birch sapling; or the other pole, the world of the orphanage and the Army, where rigid legalisms guided one's way to and fro with the fixity of a corral and chutes. A cow may travel parallel with the fence; she may not travel at right angles and into the fence. George had taken to heart the army adage, "Do what you're told and never volunteer." And the runways were painless to travel and impalpable to the obedient, who without question or conscious decision slept here, washed there, ate yonder, and waited.

The area which as yet completely baffles me is the sexual one. Al Williams referred to George's sexual attitude as "wholesome"; I denied it and still can't say why. Al said that because, as George so lucidly explains it in his extraordinary manuscript, George is without shame, false modesty, insecurity or hypocrisy. He has plodded along a path of unassailable logic and satisfied himself with certain truths that mankind, categorically, is unable to accept subjectively: that erection, orgasm and ejaculation are as possible to a rabbit as a man and in man, no more noble; that these phenomena need not be nurtured because they are (given a chance) automatic and unstoppable; and if it is senseless to nurture them, it is even more so to suppress them. This Al calls wholesome; well, to use George's own simile, it is precisely as wholesome as a rabbit's. The great complications of sex, which run in tides and stain man's thoughts, speech and works, are incomprehensible to George and, until he turns to look, out of Al's field of view.

The conclusion that the extraordinary bestiality of George's Rorschach reactions is sexual in nature seems at first a foregone conclusion. Extraordinary is hardly the word for it; I have conducted over a thousand Rorschachs and have read everything I could find on the technique and interpretation of the device, and never have I heard of anything like George's consistent, bloody, murderous pictorializations. Not in Rorschachs—but yes, yes indeed in deep psychoanalysis. But it is invariably found profoundly hidden, and emerges slowby and almost never directly, but symbolically.

According to George's biography, Anna is the only woman he ever knew—and I believe it. What little he says about their relationship is unclear. She apparently was the instigator; George says more than once that he did what she wanted. He then makes obscure reference to his doing what he wanted; that she tried to stop him and then permitted it, feeling safe with him.

Safe with him!

What is safe with him? Who?

Me?

Well . . . we'll have to work some more, learn some more. Fantasies of violence sometimes symbolize sex; sexual symbols (and sexual acts) often symbolize and express violence. Somewhere in this area may be theoretical room for the incredibly violent, often genital, yet virtually asexual fantasies of George's Rorschach.

Summary: April 3.

Two more long sessions with George. . . .

(. . . .it is interesting to inject here the reminder that Sergeant Outerbridge was still on the struggling staff of an overcrowded, underequipped military neuro-psychiatric hospital, carrying a tremendous load, working impossible hours. The fact that he had found six of them for George, and the lack of complaint from Col. Williams, attest to his devotion and superhuman energy.)

. . . have brought us through motor coordination tests, the house drawing, the human figure drawing, and the Thematic Apperception.

The motor coordination was the first thing we tackled after the harrowing experience of the Rorschach. It consisted of his copying eight different geometric figures composed of circles, squares, wavy lines and dots. He did them precisely, with care and planning, making corrections to improve them. It appeared that despite a compulsively rigid manner of performing, his motor control was in good order and not over-run easily by his deeper, guarded (frightened?) feelings. Watching him do it, I felt I was watching a pencil-and-paper re-enactment of each new experience he had ever had in controlled circumstances—the orphanage, the Army bases. He sought the channels between fences; he eagerly searched for the areas in which he might, once they were known, run freely without having to think. It was easy to see how he had been able to hold down two years and more of Army motor mechanics, working much of the time alone, and free to use his hands.

Reassured somewhat, I ventured a little closer to the emotional edge, always uncertain where it might begin to crumble under our feet. I asked him to draw a house.

He drew a traditional house with a formal, landscaped garden, in the artistic style of an anxious six-year old. Each window was given twenty or more panes; the flower-beds and three trees were formed by forceful, tight, tiny scrawlings in contrast to the tenuous thin lines framing the larger structure of the house. Two things stood out as grotesque: the garden he placed in midair above the first story and sprawling out into the upper wall of the house, and the roof was simply cut out of his drawing by the top of the paper. It was hardly a balanced picture. It showed poor perspective and poor planning. It suggested that he could not be counted upon for responsible handling of everyday adult reality. He ignored the fundamentals, preoccupied with his private details. He could manage in compulsive fashion if his life were kept simple, but he might otherwise go to pieces.

I drew a deep breath (silently) and told him to draw a human figure. I said *a* human figure, but he proceeded to draw a man and a woman, hurriedly, carelessly, as if, having made the outlines, he could not wait to blacken them in, which he did with a heavy hand: filled-in black legs, arms, torsos right up to the chin, then a round black hat on the woman, a square black hat on the man, close over their eyes. Cover up, cover up . . . anxiety.

He stopped and I said, "Is that all?"

To the best of my ability I said it casually and neutrally, but the heavy eaves of his eyes flicked up and he scanned my face, as avidly, for a second, as he had conned the ink-blots. There was a flicker of frown between his brows. "Can I do it over?"

"Sure."

He put his pencil to the paper, held it still, and flashed me that look again. If I believed in telepathy, which emphatically I do not, I would have testified to the receipt of an urgent, "*Can I tell?*" Then he set to work.

I thought, as I watched him, how the human psyche, especially the ill one, cries out for contact and communication. George's partial alexia—the inability to use the spoken word while he could write with such facility—was a phenomenon I had not seen before although I had heard of it. But I was thinking of all the other ways a sick soul reaches out . . . how the hand of a lonesome person remains outstretched after a handshake, deserted and seeking; how the eyes can express terror alone out of the almost sleeping face of a catatonic; how stern control of impending tears is betrayed by the puckering of the chin. I was convinced by now that George was unaware of anything unwell or odd about himself; yet I was conscious of a thing within him, alive and fully conscious of itself and of his affliction. In that momentary glance, like a separate, sentient being which had borrowed his eyes, it pleaded, "*Can I tell?* I know. *I know.* Let me tell."

George was drawing a male and a female.

They were—*pears?* I would not lean closer, and divert him; I stayed where I was and peered.

Nude. Head and shoulders together, a single sharp narrow curve. A mere suggestion of arms, perhaps held behind them. Narrow chests, the breasts of the woman indicated with a mere W-shaped zigzag. Huge, pregnant-seeming bellies, and an indeterminate squiggle for legs and feet. Just like two pears with dot-dot faces on their high narrow top-ends, and all else concentrated into that full round bulge.

Leaning very close, holding his pencil with great

care, flaring his strong nostrils again and again, he drew meticulous nipples on the caresless W of the breasts, a perfectly round, very black navel, an identical opening down at the bottom. Then he donated another perfect circle to the man for a navel.

He put down the pencil and shoved the paper across to me. He had forgotten altogether to draw sex organs for the male. I made no comment except to say that was fine, and my usual comment about how well he was doing. That young man was so starved for praise that it disappeared within him on contact, never to be heard from again.

"You can make all sorts of animals that way," he said suddenly, one of the few times he ever volunteered anything. He drew a whole row of the pear shapes, then on one he put long ears—rabbit—on another short spike ears and a stringy tail—possum—round ears and a thick ringed tail—racoon—sharp ears, whiskers and a thinner tail—cat—and so on, until he had eight different cartoon animals. "See?" he all but crowed. He even grinned for a second; I wished he would do that more often. A somber lad, altogether.

I began to rise, and then sat down again to watch him return to the drawing.

On each and every animal—they were all drawn in the same pose, sitting down, facing forward, with their round fat bellies thrust out—he was carefully drawing his small bold circular navels.

It was time to go. I collected the papers and hammered on the door for the guard.

●

April 9.

I have just returned from an hour and a half on Thematic Apperception. And if I found it possible to laugh at the ludicrous defenses a psyche can put up, I'd roar.

George's alexia, his difficulties with the spoken word, disappeared like magic for the Thematic Apperception, and when I reasoned out why, I marveled.

The test is simply a series of pictures, the kind of thing one sees in magazine illustrations, but carefully chosen to present a number of pivotal and interpersonal stiuations. For example, one might be a picture of a girl standing in the open door of a cabin. One patient says she is going out; one that she is going in; another that she has been standing there all day waiting for someone. On occasion a tremendous amount of contributory detail comes tumbling out: the girl's name, the presence or absence of persons in the cabin behind her, and their impending actions; sometimes the comb in her hair or her "new shoes" will be the central factor. Obviously these spur-of-the-moment stories and anecdotes relate to the patient. Frequently they serve as surrogate solutions to a patient's own problems, solutions the patient dare not face personally, as for example a girl who is in an agony of indecision about leaving home might react to the picture with a tale of a girl who left and was horribly murdered, or a girl who did not leave and got so mad she killed her father.

It came to me, listening to George incredibly chattering on and on over the pictures, that his verbal censor sat upon the subject of himself. As he remarked in his biography, there is always likely to be someone listening who doesn't hear right and will get you wrong. It would seem that he was afraid to be heard aright; that is, his mouth might give something away when he wasn't looking. And give away what? Possibly some anecdotes for which he feared he might get punished (though I am morally certain he feels no guilt) but much more likely he wished to conceal feelings and conclusions and observations which would attract the attention and derision of other people. Incapable of evaluating like other people, he was incapable of knowing before he spoke the effect his words might have.

But in the face of Thematic Apperception, his censor gave one relieved sigh and went to sleep. For it was—it must have been—convinced that as long as George talked within the four corners of a picture, he could not talk about himself!

He talked about himself—fluently, boldly, and never knew it. And the peak of the ludicrous (if one could laugh) came when amongst the pictures appeared a white blank card with a border around it—a picture for the patient to make up himself and talk about. And when George came to it his censor awoke and restored to him his soft growling slur: "A blank one? . . . nothing. It would probably be about myself. No story."

But the ones about other people? . . . these are verbatim.

A boy and a woman standing in a room: "The kid used to do a lot of stuff, he got sent away. He was away so long him and his mother don't hardly know what they look like. He just come back. In a minute she is going to put out her arms and he will run to her and she will squeeze him real hard but the front of her dress is not soft. It's full of rocks. And it isn't his mother but somebody dressed up in the mother's clothes is going to steal the money."

A boy standing by a window. A shotgun leaning against the wall. "Let's say a kid is in a shack. A window and shotgun there. He has been reading up on doctor books, operations and all. His father is going to get operated on. He is going to go to the hospital and stand there and tell that doctor if he makes a mistake he will blow his head off. But the gun goes off and kills the father."

A man bestowing a kiss on the forehead of a silver-haired lady. "A guy is kissing his mother on the forehead. Likes her a lot. Thought about her a lot and did everything she wanted and give her a kiss like that every night or so. I could go on further but–she died. The guy went all to pieces. He wanted to go to the grave and fix it all up with flowers. He always felt better if he was around her grave. That's why I would like to get out of here. No one takes care of my mother's grave and father's grave too. I always did."

(Interesting wish(guilt?)-fantasy; he has never seen his father's grave.)

A man lying asleep on a grassy bank. "I'd say probably somebody beat this guy up. Killed him. He's going to drag his body out of the way so no one would see. Behind some tanks or something. He probably killed to get his money. He cut him too. Then he went off in the woods and I guess he will do it again some time in some other place."

Boys swimming in an "ole swimmin' hole." "Oh, well one of those kids got a bad leg and it starts to bleed, and so one of the other kids comes up to see and the kid that is hurt starts to scream and the other kid can't stand that so he pushes him under and that ends that. Then the other kid comes out of the water. He was lost before but now he knows where he is."

Bland and unemphasized, cheerful and inventive, George talked on and on: theft, murder, mayhem, mother-death, father-death father-murder; drownings, stabbings, operations. No seduction, rape, adultery. No (in in the conventional sense) happiness, though George, in most instances, seemed far from sad. The dying mothers sobered him a little.

A letter.

Cackle College
Thalamus, Ore.

O-R
April 9

Dear Phil:

You sent your report on your Man in the Iron Mask with your usual deft timing, just when I was about to utter a long-range howl about it.

I will concede that it is all very fascinating, and that you were right in intuiting—if it was intuition—that there was a good deal more to that young man than met the eye. But Phil—I have to tell you, word got back to me about that little occasion you had on your third floor. A violent case should not have been put there where he had to double up with another patient. Even a potentially violent one. Yet you put him there because you had no free solitaries on the fourth floor, right?

Right.

And you were away at the time. Sick leave! Phil—are you all right? . . . but all the same, you weren't there.

Nothing came of it this time but there can be others; there will. Now I'm way on your side about your George, and you've dredged up a whole mess of internal garbage, and he's sicker than I thought he was. *But*—get him out of there.

To end on a different note, thanks for sending George's drawings along with the report. Very interesting, as my dear old mother used to say. (She used to say it at art galleries, every time. It's something to say, and it hurts no one's feeling no matter what.) But what interested me even more, my head-shrinking friend, is your identification of all those succulent shapes as pears.

Granted we all have our preoccupations . . . but to

me the little animal on the end is nothing in the world but a titmouse.

Pears indeed. You want the name of a good doctor? Or are you becoming a vegetarian?

Al

And the answer:

Manor Depressive, O-R
Dementia, Cal. April 11

Dear Al:

It might seem small of me to pull rank on you, and it's damn rude, I know, to quote a guy's compliment back at him; but you yourself once said that professionally I outrank you six ways from Sunday, or some such. And, Al, it is my considered opinion that our George is potentially more dangerous than anything else in the place.

I'll forestall your demand: can I prove it? by conceding that I can't. I just *know*, that's all. Nobody could boil off the stuff he does without being loaded and armed, and if he goes bang, I want it to be in top security.

Now it could be that what he's got is dangerous like a sword and not like a gun or a bomb. Thing is, I don't know yet what kind of thing it might be. I will, and I think soon; but until I do I'd as soon turn a Bengal tiger loose in the halls.

Leave me commit the further enormity of reminding you that I have been right so far.

They are so pears. But I admit it is subject to spelling changes.

You could be right.

Phil.

P.S. No, damn you, I wasn't sick. I confess I went to the

Big Town and credentialed myself into the cell under the library where they keep the really sensational doity books. Just to irritate you, I enclose my notes.

P.O.

A sheaf of handwritten notes on yellow paper.

von Krafft-Ebing, the old peeper . . . walking around the hind end of the nineteenth century, tattling. Had no use for Freud. By him, everything "hereditary taint." "Bore out his fixed idea that there are certain things *nice* people don't do. But indefatigable researcher all the same so shaddup keep yr prejudices to yrslf.

LUST-MURDER

Lust potentiated as cruelty, murderous lust extending to anthropophagy. Boy what a litry style von K-E had . . . lookit:

"1827. Leger, vine-dresser, aged twenty-four. From youth moody, silent, shy of people. He started out in search of a situation. Wandering about eight days in the forest he there caught a girl twelve years old, violated her, mutilated her genitals, tore out her heart, ate of it, drank the blood, and buried the remains. Arrested, at first he lied, but finally confessed his crime with cynical cold-bloodedness. He listened to his sentence of death with indifference and was executed. At the post mortem examination, Esquirol [who he?]* found morbid adhesions between the cerebral membranes and the brain.

"Vincenz Verzeni, born in 1849 in Spain; since Jan. 11, 1872, in prison; was accused (1) of an attempt to strangle his nurse Marianne, four years ago, while she lay sick in bed; (2) of a similar attempt on a married woman, Arsuffi, aged twenty-seven; (3) of an attempt to strangle a married woman, Gala, by grasping her throat

*"Famous nineteenth century psychiatrist.

while kneeling on her abdomen; (4) on suspicion of the following murders: . . ."

[Well, most of these don't matter, but here's one:]

"In December a fourteen-year-old girl, Johanna Motta, set out for a neighboring village between seven and eight o'clock in the morning. As she did not return, her master set out to find her, and discovered her body near the village, lying in a path in the fields. The corpse was frightfully mutilated with numerous wounds . . . The nakedness of the body and erosions on the thighs made it seem probable that there had been an attempt at rape; the mouth filled with earth, pointed to suffocation. In the neighborhood of the body, under a pile of straw were found a portion of flesh torn from the right calf and pieces of clothing. The perpetrator of the deed remained undiscovered.

"When caught, Verzeni confessed to this and many other murders. He was then twenty-two years old, bull-necked. . . . [Oh-oh. Here we go on the Krafft-Ebing hobby-horse] . . . as seemed probable, Verzeni had a bad ancestry—two uncles were cretins, a third, microcephalic . . . The father showed traces of pellagrous degeneration . . . his family was bigoted and low-minded [!] . . . there was nothing in his past that pointed to mental disease, but his character was peculiar"

[He'd probably describe the Marquis de Sade as downright odd.]

". . . Verzeni was silent and inclined to be solitary. . . . admitted the murders gave him an indescribably pleasant (lustful) feeling, which was accompanied by erection and ejaculation. As soon as he had grasped his victim by the neck, sexual sensations were experienced. It was entirely the same to him, with reference to these sensations, whether the women were old, young, ugly, or beautiful. Usually simply choking them had satisfied him.

"But in the case of the girl, Johanna Motta, and, it was discovered later, other women, he had done more. The abrasions of the skin on Johanna's thigh were caused by his teeth whilst sucking her blood in most intense, lustful pleasure.

"These statements of this modern [to Krafft-Ebing, modern, that is] vampire seem to rest on truth. Normal sexual impulses seem to have remained foreign to him. Two sweethearts that he had, he was satisfied to look at; it was very strange to him that he had no inclination to strangle them or press their hands, but he had not had the same pleasure with them as with his victims.

"Verzeni stated in his confession, "I had an unspeakable delight in strangling women . . . It was even a pleasure only to smell female clothing . . . I took great delight in drinking Motta's blood. It also gave me the greatest pleasure to pull the hairpins out of the hair of my victims . . . after the commission of the deeds I was satisfied and felt well. It never occured to me to touch or look at the genitals or such things. It satisfied me to seize the women by the neck and suck their blood. To this very day I am ignorant of how a woman is formed. During the strangling and after it, I pressed myself on the entire body without thinking of one part more than another."

[Backing off from the sheer horror of it, it strikes one how Verzeni's indifference to his genitals, his failure to think of a woman's body as having parts and the sucking of blood—all child-like, infantile, like a wildly hungry baby.]

And a response:

Base Hospital HQ
Office of the Administrator — O-R
Portland, Ore. — April 12

Phil:

All right, I'll stand by my compliment since I meant it, at least at the time. I'll give you an indefinite but short extension in the matter; so whatever you plan to do about it you'd better do. Because the next time I mention it there will be no arguments.

A. W.

P. S. Your library notes range all the way from distasteful to disgusting, and fail to make your case.

April 14: Therapy session. Forenoon.

Q. George, you trust me, don't you?
A. Uh-huh, I guess.
Q. Why do you suppose it's so hard to talk to you?
A. Is it?
Q. Remember when we were doing the Thematic–you know, the pictures where you made up the stories? You were talking a blue streak.
A. Don't rightly remember.
Q. If you could talk straight to me like that, we'd get through real fast.
A. Well I could try.
Q. Attaboy! Man, I *like* working with you. Okay, let's go. . . . George–
A. Hm?
Q. What was in the letter you wrote Anna overseas?
A. –
Q. George?
A. –
Q. George, I thought you were going to help.
A. Well I just don't remember. (Very surly.)
Q. Okay, we'll forget that. George, when you go hunting–
A. Ah-h-h. . . . not that again.
Q. (After a long pause.) You see how something makes you clam up? George, that something's no friend of yours. That something doesn't want you to leave here.

A. (Plaintive.) Well I just can't *help* it.
Q. (Warmly as possible.) I know you can't, George. . . . *I* can, though.
A. You can what?
Q. I know a way to help you remember better so you can talk better.
A. How? (Warily.)
Q. Take off your shoes.
A. My *shoes?* (But takes them off.)
Q. Attaboy. Now lie down on the cot. No, on your back.
A. (Reluctantly.) Well—all right.
Q. Close your eyes. . . . You're all tensed up. Relax your hands. That's it. Make your feet go limp.
A. You going to make me go to sleep?
Q. No. That's a promise. You'll be awake the whole time and every minute you'll know you can get right up and stop it if you want to. Close your eyes again. That's it. Now the hands, the feet. You are not sleepy, you're just relaxed, limp all over. Feel how limp your toes are, your ankles. No, don't move 'em! Just let them go limp; feel how limp. Now that same limpness is in the calves of your legs and your knees, they're like oiled they're so limp. Unwind that fist, there, feel your fingers—no, don't move 'em. The thumb is One, the pointer is Two; now feel each one go limp as I count them, One Two Three Four Five. One Two Three Four Five. One Two—how do you feel?
A. (Subdued.) Pretty good. Very good. Like on my aunt's farm.
Q. Now I'm going to show you just how well you can remember. I bet I can make you remember something you forgot and didn't even know you'd forgotten. . . . George, can you remember a happy time when you were a little boy? Say when you were four years old. Four years old. Four years old. Remember a quiet time

in the kitchen at home, maybe? Before our mother was very sick?

A. (Contentedly.) Mmm . . .

Q. You are four years old. In the kitchen at home. Four years old. Does your head come up to the top of the table?

A. (Wonderingly) N-no . . .

Q. Is it warm in the kitchen when you are four years old?

A. Warm.

Q. Now look around you. Slowly. Look on the shelves. Look at the chair. Look at the cracks in the floor. Look around you, four years old. Look at what you forgot all these years. Look along the window sill. Look around your . . .

A. (Quiet, absolute astonishment.) There's . . . my . . . *plate!* (Leaps off the cot, bolt upright, face inflamed, mouth open. Laughing. Shouts:) I seen my goddam *plate!*

Q. You did?

A. Look, when I was a little kid I had a plate, it was blue around the edge and white inside, down in the bottom was a blue picture of a cow. Why, I didn't think of that goddam plate now since the whale puked up Jonah!

Q. Well, *good!* Now get back on the cot.

A. I seen it so good I seen the craze around the edge near the top.

Q. Shh. Relax now and close your eyes. This is a kind of game, and one of the rules is that if I put you back to four years old I have to bring you out again. Shh now. . . . Now you are four years old, in the kitchen. Feel how warm in the kitchen, four years old. You're just a little boy four years old. Now stand there in the kitchen but don't look for anything. Just feel warm. Now in a minute I'm going to clap my hands. As soon as you hear the handclap you will be twenty-three. You will be twenty-three right here and now in the room with me. I'm going to count backwards from five to one and then clap my hands. Understand?

A. Mmm . . .

Q. Five, Four, Three, Two, One. (Clap.) Okay. You can open your eyes. How do you feel?

A. Like I slept two hours. Phil, what did you do?

Q. It's just a remembering trick. You do it just fine.

A. That is the damndest thing I seen yet. My plate, you imagine?

Q. I'm glad. . . . Close your eyes.

A. You going to do it again?

Q. Not right away. But you are so comfortable now. Take it easy, like the feller says. You're taking it easy. Easy.

A. Yeah.

Q. They feed you all right?

A. Feed good. I had worse and paid for it.

Q. You take it easy, easy like that, you can talk real good to me, you know that?

A. I guess.

Q. You like the movies?

A. I didn't see no movies in a long time. Yes, I like movies.

Q. What kind you like best?

A. Western movies.

Q. So do I. . . . George, you know how you can always tell the good guy from the bad guy?

A. Sure. If the good guy gets shot it's always in the chest or shoulder and if the bad guy gets shot it's always in the belly.

Q. (Laughs. A lot.) By God George. I never knew that! And you know, now I think of it, you're right? I was going to say about moustaches.

A. Oh yeah, that.

Q. George, close your eyes. Take it easy, easy now. I want you to remember a bad time you had but I want to see if you can remember it easy, easy.

A. Oh . . . Okay.

Q. Close your eyes. Take it easy. I want you to remember when they sent for you and you went to see the major, the one had your letter. George, you've got a frown right there over your nose. Iron it out. You can't take it easy with a frown over your nose. Good. Oh, *real* good. Now I just want you to remember that time, and how it was. How you felt. How mad you were. When you took the glass. When you broke the glass.

A. (Suddenly raises and clenches right hand. Muscles knot under the shirt. Face twists. Breath hisses.)

Q. You never got the chance, George. What did you want to do then? Suppose you'd had the chance, nobody around by you and him?

A. Kill 'im. I'd 'a killed 'm.

Q. How? What would you do? What would he do?

A. I'd take that broken glass or a knife, I'd let 'im have it. He—

Q. Go on.

A. He'd back off but I'd go after him. I'd cut a big hole and the blood would jump out all over the place.

Q. Mm-hm. And then . . .

A. And then the old man would look at me like he didn't know what hit him. He'd go nuts. His eyes pop out, scared to death . . . It wouldn't do him no good if he was mad at me now. He's so weak. He can't stand up no longer. Before you know it he's on the floor, choking, like he can't breathe. He shakes his head back and forth a minute . . . That's it. He finally got his!

Q. (!) And what then, George?

A. I guess that's all. He wouldn't bother me no more. He'd leave my mother alone now, too.

Q. Yeah.

A. Yeah.

Q. George . . . Did you ever see a man die that way, with the blood jumping out all over the place?

A. (Without hesitation.) That old watchman. By the paper box factory.

Q. Was it an accident?

A. Hell no. I hit him over the head with a pipe first. I must have knocked him cold because he didn't put up no fight. Or maybe he was too drunk. Then I cut his chest like a damn rabbit. The old bum didn't have much blood.

Q. George, where did you cut him? Show me exactly where you put the knife.

A. Right here. (Grasps his chest with his right hand between the right nipple and the armpit.)

Q. What did you do after the old man died?

A. I pushed him behind the big tank.

Q. And then what did you do?

A. I went back into the woods. But it was too dark to do anything. I got lost a while, I guess. (He pushes his hands flat under his belt and down inside his trousers.) Get hot thinking about it.

Q. Hot? You mean for a woman?

A. (Snorts.) O God no! Here—*here!* (He is clutching his lower belly.)

Q. What happens when you get hot like that, George?

A. I like to hunt. Rabbit, look out.

Q. Like hungry.

A. It's different.

Q. (Looks at watch.) Which reminds me, I better cut out of here or I won't get any lunch. Missed the first two shifts already.

A. Me too, I wish I had a horse let alone rabbit.

Q. (Knocks on door for guard.)
A. Hongry hongry hongry!
Q. Take it easy; easy now.
A. You got me all churned up, Phil.
Q. (Pounds on door.)
A. They all gone to lunch. Nobody but you and me here now.
Q. (Pounds on door.)
A. (Kneading lower belly.) Turble to feel like this, you cain't kill yourself a possum or a rabbit.
Q. You just take it easy, George. . . . here's Gus now. Gus, I thought you'd never get here!

Comments: This is the day, the breakthrough, and man, man, man, the number of times I almost blew it. (Later) Had to go for a walk and come back. Too excited to write for a while. Now let's see where we suddenly are.

First of all, George's suggestibility. I don't know why, but I am always surprised when some shingle-bundled busted-hinge ego turns out to be a good hypnotic subject. Clinical data bear it out and I should not be amazed, but I always am. You always think the integrated phlegmatic type is going to go under easiest. Why, George slips under like a saucer in a dishpan. And he regressed, at least in light trance, to four years old as if he had a head start.

Next was the experiment to see if the trance episode had increased rapport between us in the waking state. That was another time I almost tipped everything over with one wild whoop of joy. He chatters like a lil ole jaybird.

And then there was the test of Ferenczi's "forced fantasies"–catching up a wish, no matter how casual or ardent, and leading the patient to the next step and the next until, like any good natural function, the wish-fantasy is achieved and peace settles in. Peace would have settled in if it hadn't been for that undignified scramble for lunch. For a while I thought it was going to be the peace you rest in.

But of course the most important achievement today

was the watchman episode. What a perfectly beautiful (clinically speaking, of course!) slide that was, effortlessly from the major to the father image to the old watchman . . . come to think of it, it's right there in George's autobiography. Will look that up. I bet it's there to be read. I bet there are other things to be read in it now that we know the language . . . and George will fill in the gaps for us.

Got to write to Al.

•

A letter.

Cuckoo Cavern
Glandular, Ore.

O-R
April 16

Well, Phil!

If you say I told you so I'll punch you right in the —on the other hand I haven't the heart. I'll say it for you; you told me so; you told me and told me. And God, when I think of the pressure I put on you: throw the bum out, I said. Give him to the waiting world, I said.

In all seriousness, congratulations, Philip. You did a superb job at wicked odds, and for as much as I was in your way I apologize.

I've contacted Lucy Quigley. Ever meet her? She was for a long time with the Regional Red Cross. She's on her own and available for a little job for us, and is willing, damned able, and almost ready.

I've asked her to go down to George's home town and root around in the newspaper files for information about that watchman's death.

If any. Now don't get mad, Phil; but you know better than I that this could be a fantasy. If there was such a death, and if it checks with what he says, it's a feather in your cap, of course. If there was no such death, or if it doesn't check out according to George's description, then it's something he heard about and appropriated. So hold your breath, kid; this is the big checkout.

Meanwhile she's going to interview Anna too. She's capable as all git-out, as I've said, and tactful and kind as well. She'll be leaving in a couple of days, so if there's anything you want asked of anyone in the area, or checked up on, fire it up here.

You know what you are, you're a detective, that's what.

Al

Base Hospital #2 O-R
Smithton Township, Cal. April 18
(I don't feel funny this afternoon.)

Dear Al:

A little weary and shook up as I write this: I think the enclosure will explain why. It was fascinating to do and I never want to do it again. My warmest regards and thanks to Miss Quigley; tell her I will be waiting, like the cat that ate the cheese and sat down by the mousehole, with baited breath.

yrs.
Phil

Enclosure:
Therapy, April 16.
(Light trance induced at the outset. Achieved without resistance and rapidly.)

Q. Quite comfortable, George?
A. Oh yeh.
Q. Feel good this morning?

A. Mm.

Q. Remember what I once said about this work we're doing, it's like bricks, and the [illegible] get and lay, the sooner we'll be finished?

A. I never forgot that.

Q. Well, George, this is going to be it. This will be the biggest load of bricks so far. What I hope for when we are through is to know you so well that anything else we do will be clear and straight and easy, right to the end of the road. That means out of here for you.

A. I hear you.

Q. You know the story of your life you wrote. You said it had in it everything you can remember.

A. It does.

Q. You know now you can remember things you didn't even know you had forgotten.

A. Oh gosh yes. My plate.

Q. That's right. Well, I have your story here and there're a couple of holes in it. You'll plug 'em for me, won't you?

A. If I can.

Q. No matter what?

A. Mm-hm.

Q. When did you start drinking blood?

A. –

Q. George?

A. –

Q. (Quietly and as kindly as possible.) Ah, George, George. Do you know that I understand how you feel? That I know what I have just done to you? . . . That was your big secret, wasn't it, George? You told yourself that somehow, if anyone ever found out it would be the end of you. You kept that secret like keeping a life.

And now it's out. And you're so scared you don't know what to do. . . . But you're not dying. This isn't the end of the world. That secret has dragged you down so much that . . . well, some day you'll know. Some day you'll know. You'll know when you get up there, how far down you've been dragged. But you can't know until you get up higher than you are. . . . Now you are getting mad, hey George? Go ahead if you want to. It's a little like the major who had your letter, isn't it? But you know who you were mad at then, you were mad at old George because you thought you'd let your secret slip out. You didn't really; and George, the letter's lost. Nobody has ever seen it but the major and one censor and they got killed, George. . . . And you didn't tell anyone this time either. I guessed it, and then I started figuring, and it added up. But I'll bet there's nobody else in the world could've guessed it. You didn't tell. *You didn't tell.* Get mad if you want but don't get mad at George. (Long pause. Finding, filling pipe. Lighting.) Now let me tell you something about secrets. There were some people a while back used to hang on to money, bury it, worry about it, even shoot people who accidentally came near it. And it was Confederate money the whole time! They forgot what it was, even. Hiding it was more important than what it was. Your secret is like that. It got to be part of you, you were hiding it even when you didn't know you were. That's why you found it so hard to talk to people, you were afraid it would slip out. . . . Well it's out now, George, and nobody's going to hurt you about it. What we're going to do is find out *why* you like to drink blood. Not *if* you do. And do you know what good it's going to do to find that out? It's so *you* will know why. Helping you find out, I'll get to know too, but I know lots of things. I'm a doctor. I keep things to myself. I wouldn't use it to hurt you. . . . I'm going to make *you* tell *you* why you drink blood. Then once you understand about it, you and I together are going to pick up all the pieces and make a new life for you. Are you asleep?

A. No.

Q. This is a whole lot to take in all at once, isn't it.

A. Mmm.

Q. Well, let's get to work. Here I have your story that you wrote. Don't open your eyes. Just take it easy. Lie quiet, quiet, quiet. Let it get dark inside your eyes. Ride the dark like a big mattress, George. Let yourself sink down into the dark, down deeper, deeper, deeper. Don't sleep. Just lie there in the warm dark. Everything's easy, easy. You hear me, you can talk, easy, easy, easy . . . About the hunting. You wrote a whole lot about the hunting but you never even once said you drank the blood of the animals you killed. You—

A. *Anyám!*

Q. What?

A. It means Mother.

Q. Go on.

A. That's all.

Q. (Pause.) You don't have to tell me if you don't want to, but why did you say that just then?

A. You asked me.

Q. I did?

A. When I started.

Q. Oh. Oh. Drinking blood. Mother. Mother?

A. She all the time said that. She said it right up to the time she died, I was so big and all . . . ah you drank the very blood out of me, she said when she felt bad. . . . Well I didn't mean to.

Q. Sure you didn't. Aw, George, that was just what they call a figure of speech, like "as the crow flies," you don't really expect a crow to be there flying. There are no horses in horseradish.

A. No, my old man told me I really did. She nursed me when I was born, when she got some sort of trouble and her breasts got to bleeding she wouldn't stop. She said it was her duty, she near died of it. She did die of it finally.

Q. (Performing what he derided in others as the Psychiatrist's Pounce; heroically, however, eliminating the A-ha! that goes with it.) You think you're responsible for that!

A. No I don't and it wouldn't make no difference, it was what she wanted, she said that and said it. She look down her nose at strong healthy mothers. She said they didn't give much. Not like her. She liked to think about that and talk about it. If she was alive today to see what happened she would be happy she died of it.

Q. You seem to have understood her very well.

A. She all the time talked about it.

Q. When did you start getting blood outside?

A. –

Q. George?

A. I'm thinkin'.

Q. Take your time.

A. . . . (Trace of anxiety.) You want to know the very first time. What if I can't remember what it was?

Q. It doesn't matter exactly the first time. Were you very small?

A. I guess so 'cause I can't remember it. I remember the cat. . . .

Q. Want to tell about it?

A. . . . kittens. It had little kittens. They was sucking on the cat. I must've been pretty small. Maybe three, four. I thought I could too. I wanted it. I remember I wanted it.

Q. . . . What happened?

A. I tried to, the cat scratched me in the face. I had this piece of auto leaf spring in my hand, I don't know how, I hit out and killed the cat dead right there. Then it couldn't stop me. But somehow it was the blood I was eating when he . . .

Q. . . . . Go on. You said, when he.

A. . . . The old man. He come up behind me hit me with his fist middle of the back. (Vaguely moves shoulders on cot.) By God I can still remember how my head snapped all the way back I seen his face upside down it was like getting struck by lightning.

Q. What did he say?

A. He didn't say nothing. He just said to quit it.

Q. I bet you can remember exactly what he said.

A. Now how could I? I was only a . . . well . . . wait a minute. (Long pause. Then, in amazed tone:) He hollered out, DON'T LET ME EVER CATCH YOU DOING A T'ING LAK DOT. Just like that.

Q. Whew. . . . So he didn't tell you not to do it.

A. Now what else?

Q. I said, *he did not tell you not to drink blood.* He said not to get caught at it. It's not the same thing at all.

A. It means the same thing.

Q. Think it over. I'll wait.

A. Jesus.

Q. George, I read in an old book–a book written maybe a hundred and fifty years ago–a story about a boy and his big brother and they stopped for the night at an inn. And there was an old man sitting by the fire and they got talking to him, and the old man said something–I don't remember what, and it doesn't matter–something very wise. And just as he said it the big brother hauled off and knocked the little boy clear across the inn.

A. What for?

Q. He said he wanted the kid to remember for the rest of his life what the old wise man said. So that's been known for a long time. You remember times like that, you remember them all the way down deep. Also you remember everything else about it as well. I bet every time you get the taste of blood in your mouth there's a big loud something, somewhere, yelling don't let me catch you.

A. Especially cats. . . . I don't like the taste.

Q. Know why?

A. By God I do.

Q. Now we know everything but why you like to drink blood.

A. I just like it.

Q. Any other reason?

A. No . . . Except sometimes I think it makes me near my mother. Don't you laugh at me.

Q. I never did yet, George, and I never will. . . . You know one thing that comes through to me when I read this story of yours is that there are times when you have to have blood and times when you can take it or leave it alone and times when you can go up to two years and never even think of it.

A. That's so, I guess.

Q. Well, what makes that?

A. I dunno.

Q. Let's have a look. Here—no: here. Hm. Times you did without were your first two years at the school and your first two or so years at your aunt's farm.

A. And in the Army.

Q. Yes, in the Army. Except—well, never mind that now. Now let's see times you had to hunt animals. The third year at the school, right? And overseas.

A. Anna got sick. Woo.

Q. A bad one, hm?

A. Woo.

Q. Well, let's look at the school one. Because nothing changed on the surface, did it? You went right on doing the same things in the same place. What happened?

A. After two years? The old man died.

Q. And that made you suddenly want blood?

A. I dunno. I just—did, is all.

Q. Maybe because with him gone you wanted that feeling of being closer to your mother?

A. That could be. It don't sound right somehow. Or it was part of it but only a little part.

Q. And nothing else happened to you around that time?

A. Mm-mm. Nup.

Q. Well, let's go on to—

A. Wait. . . . Maybe this . . . (A long pause.) I tell you, after the old man died everything was way different. Like when I would get out I would have him to go back to. He wasn't nothing to me, but there wasn't nothing else.

There sure was not one single thing in that dump of a town to go back to. With him gone I was like lost.

Q. Then whenever you felt sort of lost, that's when you wanted blood.

A. You get hot in the stomach.

Q. It happened when Anna got sick and when your father died and when you got shipped overseas.

A. And a whole lot at home with old man, him drinking. And when Uncle Jim beat up on me that time with the skunk and told me don't come back don't come back.

Q. So there you go, George: did you ever know before that your desire for blood came from outside you, by the things that happened to you, and not from inside really at all?

A. No I never.

Q. And now you know when you get that hot stomach you can take care of it some other way than killing something to get its blood. You know that something's making you feel lost, and if you go fix that, you won't need the blood. Not ever.

A. And I always thought I needed it and I was the only one.

Q. You've just been looking at the wrong end of the thing. There may not be many who have to drink blood, but there are millions—billions, even, who feel what you feel that makes you drink blood.

A. I don't get you.

Q. Everyone on earth feels lonely sometimes, lost sometimes. Just the way you do. Everybody has his own way of handling it, just as you had a way.

A. I always thought I was the only one.

Q. Don't think it any more. . . . Hey, here's another hole in your story. You say here you broke into the funeral home the night they laid your mother out there. What for?

A. What'd I write? To say good-bye.

Q. 'To say good-bye to her in his own way,' is what you wrote. What is your own way of saying good-bye?

A. (After a long pause.) She always said it was for me.

Q. (Carefully.) Tell me what it was like in there.

A. Well it wasn't no fancy place, not in that town. Just a big workroom kind of place, shelves and sinks and like that, and she was on a long table with a sheet over her and her face. They taken all the blood out of her. I seen them do it at night through the window blind in the back a hole. It was in a bottle on the floor.

Q. And you–

A. She always said that's what it was for. And in a way it made us be like part of each other forever, don't you laugh at me.

Q. I'm not laughing. . . . All right, George. We'll go on. . . . Here's something. You mention a quarry on the other side of town where there were big frogs.

A. Sometimes frogs are good, like on a real hot day, like for a change. They are cold you know. Especially if you scare 'em off where they're sunning and they dive down deep and hide. They can stay down ten, fifteen minutes and when they come up they're real cold. Only thing is the biggest frog you ever saw isn't but a mouthful's worth. A frog can't see you if you don't move. You wait where you chase 'em, they will come right back practically into your hand if you know how to sit still.

Q. You know you're a regular nature guide, George. I never met a man who knew so much about small game hunting.

A. Well I studied at it.

Q. Oh yes—here's that part you wrote about sex. You have a very good head on you, George. A lot of people who are supposed to be smarter than you and me put together haven't figured the thing out as neatly as you did. But tell me something—is Anna the only girl you ever had?

A. Uh-huh.

Q. Look, you won't mind telling me. When you and Anna—

A. Phil, I don't want to get you mad—

Q. Go ahead. What were you—

A. What's that you—

Q. (Laughs.) Now don't everybody talk at once. What did you say?

A. Phil, don't ask me about Anna and me, how we do it, all right?

Q. If it's important to you not to talk about it, we won't.

A. Well thanks. I got to tell you, I been sort of holding off talking all this time because I wanted us to get past that.

Q. Anything like that on your mind, speak up right at the beginning. I'm here to work with you, not on you.

A. Well all right, there is one more thing, now that you mention it.

Q. Shoot.

A. That letter I wrote Anna, that started all this trouble. I don't want you to ask me nothing about it.

Q. (Swears, but silently.) Of course not, if you don't want me to.

A. (Lies back expansively, heaves a deep breath.) Well all right. Now anything goes.

Q. All right. Then quit bouncing around and relax all over again. Close your eyes and make it black, and sink into the black and drift in it. Don't sleep. You can hear me very well. You can talk very well. Relax all over. Toes. Ankles. Fingers. One Two Three Four Five. How do you feel?

A. (Peacefully.) Swell.

Q. I'm looking through your story again for holes. I see what you mean, George. It *is* all here, once you know how to read it. Here's the whole thing about the watchman, and I didn't even see it the first time I read it.

A. (Peacefully.) That was after the fight with Uncle Jim.

Q. Of course you didn't go into much detail . . . still, it's there. You like human blood?

A. The best I ever had was human blood. But it wasn't that ol' bum.

Q. (Hesitates.) Well, we'll come to it, I imagine. . . . Oh, here's something. About the beaver lodge.

A. Yeah and the kid tripped my deadfall.

Q. You don't say much here about what happened. Wasn't he hurt?

A. Oh, his leg was mashed some. It didn't bother him after I got there.

Q. You get him out all right?

A. I got him out all right. I beat hell out of him. I wrote it there, it was like he was that damn baby made Anna sick and I could finally hit out at it.

Q. What happened to him finally?

A. I put him in the lake.

Q. Wait a minute . . . something about a lake . . . you made up a story in the Thematic Apperception test. You remember, the picture of the swimming hole. Something about a kid screaming, another kid pushed him under the water. Yes, his leg was hurt too.

A. Well yes, it happened like that.

Q. You cut him, George?

A. After I got him back out. He was dead then. It didn't hurt him.

Q. How old a boy was it?

A. I don't know nothing about kids, how old they are for how big. Six, seven, something like that. That was the one I told you, best I ever had. But I was so mad at him, I had a chance to hit back. That probably made all the difference.

Q. Where did you cut him?

A. Through the belly-button.

Q. Whose kid was he?

A. God, I dunno. Them Pollock families up that way got more kids than they can count and the dumb bastards can't count so much either. This wasn't from around my way, Phil. This was up to'rds Cravensville. Matter of fact Cravensville is right on that same lake, but on the other side and around the point from where I was.

Q. What did you do with him after?

A. Just dropped him in the lake like he drowned.

Q. George, you enlisted right after that. The very next day. Was that because you were scared about the kid?

A. Yes and no. I knew I was heading for big trouble the way I was. I wasn't worried about that one, it was the next one or the one after I was worried about, if you see what I mean. You could get careless. And I made a guess the Army would be about like the school only bigger and I was right. It straightened me out for two, three years until they shipped us out.

Q. Question of being lost or not lost, again.

A. You're so right. Nobody was as lost as me after we carried those stretchers off those C-119's. I seen where I was going and it was that. I seen where I been and it was gone. Something had to give.

Q. It did. . . . Oh, I have a note here I wanted to ask you about, George. Something rubbed me a little as I slid past the first reading, and stubbed me the second time around. A little thing but when you describe something, I always know where everything and everybody is. But in this one place where your father came home drunk and you had the knife.

A. Oh yes.

Q. Let me read this out loud. It's where you threw the knife. Right across the room, correct? Yes. Well, listen: ". . . he looked down at the cut and the blood coming from it. And the mother was bleeding through her hands and her eyes bulging out over them, looking at the father. And the father pushed George away and got the dishrag . . ." and so on.

A. Yes, well what about it?

Q. If you threw the knife from across the room, how was it your father pushed you away? I got the feeling the father just stood there, apparently near the sink, so he didn't move toward you.

A. Oh, it was me moved. (Suddenly quiet and intense.) It was like nothing that ever happened to me before or since. The knife stuck in his chest muscles, I don't think it passed a rib. It just stuck there. And then when he pulled it out I walked across there like I was pulled by a wire, like a sleep-walker in the movies. I could no more help myself . . . I walked across there and I put my mouth on that cut and sucked on it, I was . . . trying to pull it together or make it go away or make it like it never happened or . . . or something, I don't know. Usually I have something to do with what I do even when I'm crazy mad, but I didn't that time, I just couldn't help myself.

Q. (After a pause) Well, I . . . guess that answers my question. How he could just reach out and push you away.

A. I scared him. I scared myself too. I guess that was why he walked out like that, and never after hit my mother or anybody. That . . . that sleep-walking thing, that scared me a hell of a whole lot more than throwing the knife, do you know that?

Q. I can well imagine. . . . had enough for today, George?

(Conventional routine to return patient to present-time, and close.)

Comments: A formal and complete evaluation will have to wait; not only is it necessary to get this information in the hands of Miss Quigley before she leaves for the South, there is too the matter of generating enough objectivity to do a fair job. Perhaps I am simply overtired, but at the moment I would disqualify myself from any necessarily clinical, impersonal analysis of these developments. Let it suffice for the moment to skim over some of the major peaks.

It would seem that the key log in the jam was the revelation to George that his secret was out. I have remarked before on the marvellous way the sick psyche shouts for help; it is a pity we can't invent a detecting device which would show which language or which instrument or which vocabulary that shout was cast in. The burden of his secrecy must have been unbearably heavy, and must have become more so of recent weeks. I am very impressed by the way in which release came to him; at the very time when I was laboriously picking my way down into the shellhole to gather him up, he was standing on the edge already working hard at the answer to my question about when he started drinking blood.

Summing up his reasons for the practice, we find that he turns to it for relief only when he is hurt, disoriented—"lost", as he puts it. This is its distinction from a usual hunger. Or to put it in another way, and using George's distinction between "satisfaction" and "relief," his blood-drinking is not like the bottled-up, raging pressures which drive the true sexual psychopath; it is much more like the demanding vacuum inside a suckling babe.

The analogy, once made, bears on the question in so many ways that it stops looking like an analogy and becomes, very nearly, an analysis. A hungry baby wants what it want with an insensate, unreasoning demand which brooks of no delay, argument, postponement or reason. In these terms it is quite fair to describe a baby's emotional nexus as insane . . . maniacal . . . obsessive. And a baby seeks his assuagement for anything else besides hunger which troubles him. When Baby bumps his head, even when his stomach is full, he can be consoled by the nipple. If he bumps his head, even when his stomach is full, and he cannot find the nipple, his outrage is enormous and his demand increases.

For anyone maltreated and denied as much as George, the transference from breast milk to blood would be understandable. In George's case it can hardly even be called a transferance—not in the light of what occurred, and what, further, he was repeatedly told, about his mother's preoccupation with her own bleeding breasts.

I am beginning to feel that George's problem is a sexual problem only in the most remote, though parallel, way. "Arrested development" is a useful phrase but in his case too wildly understated. It would seem that his emotional development absolutely ceased, not at adolescence or in pre-puberty, like so many of these cases, but in the most primitive levels of the infantile. The fact that his physical and mental development in all other areas is relatively unimpaired may be unlikely, may be statistically impossible, but remains a fact.

●

Hotel Venetian
Charlotte, North Carolina May 5

Dear Dr. Outerbridge:

"Socked in," as the airlines people call it, by fog, I have to stay here overnight and get tomorrow's plane instead. I mailed my report to Col. Williams this evening, but I don't imagine airmail will move tonight any more than I will. So with an evening on my hands and a typewriter in my luggage, I thought I'd write you, if only because I know you must be on tenterhooks awaiting the news.

Col. Williams may have told you that I was a psychiatric nurse before I was a Red Cross worker. I tell you that to add substance to my congratulations. Please do not be angry at Col. Williams for having shown me your "O-R" correspondence—he is an old friend, and he is sure, as I want you to be, that I am not the kind of "record" which that correspondence is "off."

To keep you no longer in suspense, let me tell you right at the outset that you were right all down the line. The two murders did occur, they happened at the times Col. Williams calculated from the patient's history and accounts—his enlistment, for example, and the best guess he could make for the Episode of the Skunky Uncle (whom, as you will see, I met and talked with).

The death of the watchman was reported in the newspaper and on the police blotter—and attributed to heart attack. I won't go into detail as to how I proceeded from there, except to say that the resistance I encountered was not trivial, the welcome I received was not warm, the assistance I got was not helpful, the threats I made were not small, and the feelings I left behind me were ones of great relief. In bald outline, I went to the chief of police, the local bartender who operates the chief of police, and the bartender's wife, who owns the bar and operates the bartender; and having gotten clearance from her, was able then to approach the coroner sufficiently armed to raid his files. They do indeed differ from newspaper and police reports, which did not mention the knife wound. The coroner, a perfectly unbelievable example of type-casting, even to the gold watchchain and the spitoon, offered what seemed to be a weaseling excuse for letting the fact of the knife-wound get lost; yet I do believe it to be the truth. What he said was that the watchman, a chronic alcoholic of long standing with virtually terminal kidney disease, atherosclerosis, stenosis of the mitral valve, and a forty-foot tapeworm, may well have died for a number of reasons with or without having been stabbed, and only coincidentally with having been assaulted. The main point to him (and the other local officials) was that where a victim was of no importance, the murderer unknown, clues few or absent, and suspects non-existent, there just was no good reason for putting an unsolved killing on the books. I gave him every assurance that the books would, for all of me, remain the way they were. Col. Williams can, if you want him to, give you chapter and verse on the legal position of this matter as far as you are concerned, but I think you may rest assured that if it ever comes to investigation and indictment, the mental condition of your patient will make any further action useless to anyone. This as a moral issue, might, as the saying goes, cause fights in bars, but it places itself outside the immediate province of the patient's diagnosis and treatment.

My next to move to Cravensville. It is situated just as your George described it, on a mountain lake which bends around a point, obscuring the far end from the town. I acquired a boat and crossed to what certainly looked like the geography George mentioned—a little cove and a small swamp where a brook seeps into the lake—and entering the cove I horrified a half-dozen naked boys swimming there; they drifted away into the woods like little ghosts. I cannot be sure I saw the actual flat rocks from which George made his deadfall, but if anyone wanted to make one there he certainly could. I did not see any beaver or lodge, but beaver have been there, as anyone can see who recognizes a pointed sapling-stump.

As for the death of the little boy, I had no luck at all with the newspapers. The town has no newspaper, and the nearest regional gazette, a weekly, must have gone to press shortly before the death of the child and found it not worth reporting in the next issue. Your George was chillingly right in one respect—life is a lot cheaper in certain areas of those mountains than one would like to believe. Poverty, illiteracy, and too many children are three great forces against overwhelming grief at the loss of a small life and a hungry mouth.

In addition, circumstances militated against anything sensational appearing in the death of the boy. For one thing, there is a highway bridge across the opposite end of the lake, and twice in the past three years people have died there (one a suicide, the other a traffic casualty) and their bodies have been found floating in the cove—a matter, I suppose, of prevailing wind or some sluggish circulation of the lake water. This, and the battered condition of the boy's body, made it easy for the local authorities to accept the conclusion that the boy had died elsewhere than at the cove. He was wearing bathing trunks, in which he had left home the afternoon before he died (poor little thing, I'd guess he lay in the deadfall all that night) so there was not even the evidence of his clothes near the death scene.

Specifically, his left leg and his right foot and ankle were crushed, although no bones were broken, and he had a good many bruises and contusions about the head and face. The incision on the naval was there, and though no one ventured a guess as to how exactly it came to be there, the hypothesis of a hit-run driver on or near the highway bridge seemed to cover everything quite neatly. I think you may chalk up one more credit to George's honesty, no matter what your convictions may be of truth being beauty and beauty truth.

I visited Mr. and Mrs. Grallus, the aunt and uncle, and I would not attempt to improve upon your George's talent for portraiture. If it should happen that George is ever freed, there is a niche for him there. The Gralluses are no longer young, and they are childless. I think the aunt has a genuine, though not overwhelming, affection for George, and would do a great deal for him if she could. I think Mr. Grallus would do even more, for he feels very guilty about the way he treated George, and would like to make it up to him. There isn't the slightest tinge of unselfishness in this; he just wishes he didn't feel guilty and would work hard to get rid of it. They both believe that Goerge is a "dummy"—retarded, that is; and if you and I had a nickel for everyone in this country who fails to make a distinction between the mentally ill and the mentally retarded, we could build a clinic large enough to treat them all.

Finally, I went to see Anna. Oh, poor Anna! Numb, mute, unlovely, unloved, and loving. She reminds one of a draft animal, especially a donkey, one covered with saddle-galls and surrounded by biting flies, which stands patiently waiting, with sad and beautiful eyes, for someone to water it or kick it or kill it or tell it what to do. . . . I embarrass myself a little, Sergeant Outerbridge; I'm really not given to flights of prosody, but I declare she touched me.

She (too) is just what your George described—a stocky woman with a widow's hump, heavy shoulders and rump, and surprisingly delicate hands, feet and ankles. Her face is broad and pink with a small pug nose, close-set eyes, and a sad soft mouth. Her jaw is massive and she has a double chin, though she isn't what anyone would call a fat girl. I met her weeding in a corn-patch, where they sent me from the house. I was glad to be able to talk to her out there and away from that drab, noisy ruin they refer to as a house. The word "mean" has several shades; everything about that house and inhabitants and all its surroundings defines every one of them.

I won't attempt a verbatim transcript of our conversation, and I have not, by the way, given one in my report to the Colonel. Anna's vocabulary and experience are so limited that the words express almost nothing. Yet she has had so little sympathy, tenderness, respect or understanding that a little of it went a long, long way.

That she loves George (she calls him Belly—didn't you report somewhere that his name is Bela?) there can be no question; she loves him through and through and in all dimensions. She accepted his apparent desertion of her, and his unbroken silence, in precisely the way the above-mentioned draft animal accepts a kick in the head. She has never broken stride, nor thought of it. She has gone right on with her succession of days, numbly remembering the two and a half years of George, and using them as her only diversion. She is not exactly waiting for him; to say that would be to imply hope, and she has never entertained hope about anything. But about one thing there is absolutely no doubt: should he ever come back, she will be here and she will be his if he will have her.

I was able to get fairly complete picture of their relationship—conversationally she has no skill and no defenses—and through a not too murky screen of euphemisms one could see that he made his capture so total because he was gentle. Sexually she was not innocent when he came along—there had been some drunken tumbles with some of the threshing crew that came by when the buckwheat was in, and one of the hired hands had used her with some regularity for a period. She also mentioned one Sammy, under whose ministrations she had for the first and only time enlisted help: she told her father who, she said, beat him half to death. I did not inquire as to what Sammy was to her but gather he is her elder brother. From what your George reports, he never forced himself on Anna, and convinced as she certainly is that all males are violently driven by sex and therefore violently drive, it really never occurred to her that George's diffidence was anything but enormous self-control and consideration. Seducing George required a good deal more than suggestions and availability. She had literally to perform the entire act with him. He apparently neither cooperated nor resisted, and for his disinterested complaisance, which she took to be a species of chivalry, she worships him. Evidently their coition was infrequent, occurring only when her desire became uncontrollable, but then always; he never resisted her. This alone would make it infrequent; you may add to it that she tried her best to emulate what she felt was his honorable self-denial, which cut down the frequency even more.

The only aggression he ever expressed must have been in every sense irresistible. You describe him as physically powerful, and his compulsion moved him as easily as he could move her. Anna's communicativeness slowed at this point almost to speechlessness, but did not quite stop. With an air of brisk and kindly matter-of-factness I was able to keep it moving and enable to put down the heavy (to her) burden of scandal and guilt involved in confessing what she had permitted. And when she had finally stammered out what she was sure was her shame and damnation, the poor creature closed her eyes and bent her head and stood there expecting, I think, me to spit on her and God to strike her dead.

Well, as gently as I could I gave her, in Basic English, as clear a delineation as I could of what I call the Kinsey Boon—the great gift given by Indiana's immortal to countless millions of needlessly worried people—the simple statistical statement that no matter what we do . . . we are not alone. And indeed she, like many another uninformed, non-reading, virtually non-thinking person, really did believe that what had happened between her and your patient was unique and unspeakable, and as noticeable to Heaven as a bloodspot on a white tablecloth. To learn that what had happened was fairly common and in itself unimportant—that was a revelation to her. And I even quoted Havelock Ellis (without, of course, mentioning Havelock Ellis) to the effect that any mutual act—*any* one, providing only that it was not forced by one upon the other, and was an expression of love, is moral. . . . A strange scene, me in my shiny city shoes standing on a billy hillside talking to a draft animal in a clean worn dress about the ways of ecstasy. Oh dear, it must be getting late; when I get sleepy I seem always to get purple.

The frequency of this act, you will be very interested to know, was every twenty-eight days, give or take a couple. He could sense it like an animal, and probably the same way. Like other things in his extraordinary manuscript, this too was hidden in plain sight. Didn't he say something about knowing before she did that she was pregnant, because she never kept track but he did?

Do we add this, Doctor-Sergeant Outerbridge, to other data on insanity and the moon?

Well, that's my story . . . and Sergeant, since this is a personal letter and not exactly a report, permit me a personal comment. I'll be formal enough to state first that my opinions must be regarded as opinions . . . I'm not a doctor. I'm a caseworker, a nurse, and a woman.

As all such, then, let me congratulate you. I deeply admire you and the way you handled this case, and I hope some day to meet you and shake your hand.

I think that George is one of the most tragic creatures I have ever heard of. I don't doubt that he will wind up in a learned paper or even in a book. I would like to be as sure that he will wind up a free, well man, perhaps in his own cornfield with his Anna. I don't know, of course, how you plan to treat him; but somehow there is no doubt in me as to *if* you will treat him. If there is anything I can do to help, please call on me. Please. It would be an honor to work with you and a triumph to succeed.

Please let me submit something to you (perhaps too simple; perhaps, because of factors I couldn't possibly know about, something after all nonsensical; perhaps something you've already thought of yourself and discarded): All three of the qualifications I mentioned above—the caseworker, the nurse, the woman—speak at once when I suggest that George is not a sexual psychopath at all, and therefore could not be expected to respond to any known treatment in that area. You yourself presented as a sort of trial hypothesis that emotionally he is arrested at the lowest levels of infancy, and that the true grotesquerie in the case lies in the unusual fact that he is quite fully developed in all other particulars. I think that was extraordinarily astute of you. I am well aware that modern psychiatry recognizes earlier and earlier indices of sexual activity and sexual differentiation. There was in Victorian times a widely accepted belief that until the age of ten all children, unless tainted by environment, were "innocent," a word which meant sexless angels. Yet it seems to me that this differentiation must have a beginning point and it is not at birth. It may be that sexual awareness of some sort goes back earlier than this point of differentiation, but I feel that it too does not go back as far as birth. If this is so, then there is a period in infancy when the child is, emotionally speaking, neither male nor female nor sexual entity, but simply a human infant (with all the demanding, insensate, "insane" demands you describe). I don't know if anyone has ever thought of this, but can one reasonably suppose that a girl infant demands the breast any less because she is a girl? . . . I know I'm being wildly intuitive and "female" in bringing this up, but I can't get it out of my head that you will find George's emotional quantum cowering in that area.

Colonel Williams made a pleasantry in one of his "O-R" notes to you, and very amusing it was; it was reference to George's drawings of pear-shaped animals, and his jocular conclusion was that they were mammary symbols. After laughing I began to think about them, and I recalled that George had also drawn a man and a woman with the same configuration. And I remembered, too, that George drew the woman's breasts with a single careless zigzag (i.e., not important) but at the same time went back and drew the nipples with great care. He always drew navels, as if he regarded as incomplete any rounded shape which did not have a terminal orifice of some kind.

So it occurred to me that his oh-so-humorous little sketches were possibly life as he sees life—living beings as his infantile emotional consciousness wishes they were and believes they are. Rabbits and squirrels and little boys and old watchmen—each one is a mamma, full of warm sustaining fluid. The entire organism is the mammary, and he feels this with such devotion that he even bypasses with zigzag the true breasts (though he cannot overlook the nipples) and in preference makes the whole female body, a mammary object; this aside from, apart from, and utterly discounting the fact that it is female!

This hypothesis then leads one to the surprising conclusion that in his (perfect word!) *periodic* aggressive erotic act with Anna, he was sexlessly performing an asexual function upon organ or object the sex of which was as unimportant as the gender of a bottle.

(I wonder if I could have spoken to Anna so convincingly of "acts of love" if I had thought this out at the time!)

And in the area of symbolism also is something I derived from George's startling dictum about how to tell the cowboy hero from the cowboy villain. (And that amazingly perspicacious young man is right!!) Heroes get shot in the chest. (Breast?) Villians get shot in the stomach. Query: Is it more than coincidence that his father and the watchman, whom he identified with the father, were cut in the chest, while the boy, whom he identified with the fetus which had displaced him wi[th] Anna, was cut in the navel?

Oh my goodness, look what I've done; I meant to give you the news and congratulate you and go to bed; the window is getting pink around the edges, the fog is gone, and my plane leaves in an hour. Sergeant, Doctor, Sir Philip—whatever you're called: thanks; it has been a pleasure to talk to you.

Cordially,
Lucy Quigley

A letter ...

Sir Philip's Bughouse
Praecox, Cal.

O-R
May 8

Dear Al:

I enclose the enclosed, a monumental missive from your Lucy Quigley, who is, as you in one way or another said, some chick. What does she look like?

I send it because I think you will enjoy it, although it contains reportorial information which I know you have in her formal report and therefore don't need, and some heady compliments addressed to me which you will feel I should have modestly kept to myself.

And in all seriousness, I want you to think over her hypothesis about the non-sexual, or should I say pre-sexual, nature of George's disorder. I'm in a neither-confirm-nor-deny mood about it at the moment, but it excites me and I'd like to echo when it bounces off you.

You'll be happy to know that I obeyed your orders of about five months back and got some sleep, about fourteen consecutive hours' worth, and that since then I have worked for forty consecutive hours cleaning up all the work which the sleep and my preoccupation with George caused to pile up. So everything is normal again. I've only seen George once in that time—I happened to be candling the head of a strait-jacketed neighbor on his corridor—and all I did was chat. One interchange you'll be interested in: I told him that I would respect his wish not to discuss his specific conduct with Anna, and the contents of the airmail letter which fused this bomb; I assured him further that I was about to ask him a question which he need not answer. I then asked him *why* he did not want to discuss these things.

Well, our George sat on the edge of his cot and scratched his handsome yellow head, and at length gave me a diffident smile and said, "I just wouldn't want you to think I was queer."

What's new with you?

Phil

Palace of Pathology
New Rosis, Ore.

O-R
May 10

Dear Phil:

Have read and reread Lucy's letter and return it herewith. You're quite right: she's some chick. Or was I the one said that? All right; *I'm* right: she's some chick. As to what she looks like, you can see for yourself. She's arriving here tomorrow and we'll grab a chopper and buzz down your way for dinner. Okay?

As to an opinion on her hypothesis, you will please excuse me, dear friend, but I have none, and if I had I wouldn't tell you. Please always regard me as being something like an airline ticket agent. I know how they come and go and I fix it for people to ride; but don't ask me how the new-fangled things work. So no opinion. As to clause 2 above, wherein I depose and say I wouldn't give you an opinion if I had one, leave me state here and now that I think you're a great man.

A clever man. A good man in several senses. But from

time to time I get these uneasy feelings. Every time I express opinions to you it turns out three months from now that I have ordered you to do this or permitted you to do that, and what's more you can prove it.

I have two pieces of news for you. One is that when I arrive I shall give you a little box with some costume jewelry in it, like silver bars, and a paper with a message suitable for framing, like a commission, and a paymaster's voucher retroactive to your 25th birthday. You can, if you are able, square it with your own conscience that under false colors you have been endearing yourself to George as a sergeant while actually an officer the whole time.

My other piece of news has to do with the late Major Manson, may his shade be reading over your shoulder to catch this my heart-felt apology. (Remember when I called him moo-headed and concluded that he had slapped a "psychosis unclassified: violent" on George solely because George had punched him in the nose?) Well, after his honorable deceasement, our efficient Army separated his personal effects from government issue and sent the former to his survivor, a daughter. She quite understandably let some time go by before she tackled the job of sorting his things. Among his papers was an unmailed air-letter form. I enclose it, and I think no one need wonder why that mail censor was intrigued enough to bring it to the major, nor why the major sent for George.

Skip lunch. That's an order. You and Lucy and I are going to eat up a storm.

'la vista,
Al

Enclosure: An unmailed air letter form. It bears the soldier's serial number, an APO post office address, and the designation of a combat unit. It is signed. The body of the letter, in toto, follows:

Dear Anna:
I miss you very much.
I wish I had some of your blood.

•

Close the file. You've read it all.

You are sitting in the lake of light from Dr. Outerbridge's desk lamp. It has grown late. But sit a while; you will not be interrupted by the fictional psychiatrist, who after all exists only for you, The Reader.

So place your hands on the bland smooth face of the closed file folders, and close your eyes, and quietly think.

Since this is and must be fiction, what would please you?

Dr. Outerbridge found Lucy Quigley absolutely charming, and in due course she became Mrs. Dr. Outerbridge. They worked famously together and achieved togetherness and fame. Does that make you happy?

George was turned over to a Veteran's Administration facility and his arrested emotional persona *was attacked with narcoynthesis, reserpine, electric shock and an understanding analyst, and in three years and five months he was discharged as cured. He married Anna, inherited his aunt's farm, and they live quietly near the woods and each other. He has learned to love children. Okay?*

Or if the idea of such as George still offends you, why it's the easiest thing in the world to have therapy fail and we'll wall him up forever. Or he could get killed in a prison riot, or escape and be brought down by police bullets. Would you like him shot in the chest? Or in the belly? You would? Why that: *what is he to you?*

But you'd better put the folder back and clear out. If r. Outerbridge suddenly returns you'll have to admit e's real, and then all of this is. And that wouldn't do, vould it?

Reunion
Rising Sign
Full Circle
Beginnings
Summer Samba